"Wow, I didn't know I was living with royalty," she said cheekily, taking a mocking bow.

The next moment, Cain pressed her against a tree. "If I was anyone who cared for these formalities, I'd have your head for your impertinence."

"Show-off." She smiled at him. Her body tingled with desire at his display of superiority, and she used his proximity to press a kiss to his lips. "Don't worry, I get your point. I promise I'll behave around other vampires. I won't behave when I'm alone with you, though."

Before he responded, she leaned in to kiss him again. He opened his mouth to welcome her probing tongue. When she broke free to catch her breath, he let his mouth travel down to her throat.

"What am I going to do with you?" He chuckled before sinking his fangs into her skin.

I0598336

The Waxing Moon

by

Elli Morgan

The Waxing Moon

Cover Art by *Jennifer Greeff*

The Wild Rose Press, Inc.
PO Box 708
Adams Basin, NY 14410-0708
Visit us at www.thewildrosepress.com

Publishing History
First Edition, 2022
Trade Paperback ISBN 978-1-5092-4400-3
Digital ISBN 978-1-5092-4401-0

Published in the United States of America

Dedication

To RebelGoddess13 (Kali)
for making me fall in love with vampires in the first place.

Never give up on your dreams.

Praise for The Waxing Moon

"Morgan has written a wonderfully sweet paranormal romance that takes you on an epic adventure across Europe. I recommend this story to anyone who likes a little bite in their romance."

~L. Starla, paranormal and contemporary romance author

"A gripping debut that leaves no time to catch one's breath!"

~Anna Jane Greenville, author of "The girl who was a gentleman"

"Elli Morgan blew my mind with her ability to wrap me up in this well-written story that stuck with me long after I finished."

~Lauren Biel, dark romance author

Acknowledgements

I'd like to thank my former classmate Anna for showing me it's possible for a German to publish a book in English. I don't think I'd have entertained the idea of writing a book without her inspiring example.

I am also grateful to my mum for always believing in me, no matter what I do.

Many thanks to my friends Iris and Ann Christin for listening to me rattling on about my book ideas and writing challenges during our Skype calls.

My deepest gratitude goes to my amazing beta readers—Iris, Laelia, Lauren, Lynoure, Marissa, Tracy, Timo, and Timothy. Without their feedback, my book wouldn't be what it is today.

Special thanks to my editor Lill Farrell and the whole TWRP team for turning my dream of publishing this story into a reality.

Part I

CAIN

A lost girl wanders,
led by the crescent moon's shine,
into the beast's arms.

Chapter 1

"Lilah? Here's a letter for you." Her mother's penetrating voice yanked Lilah out of her book.

"Not now, Mum." She groaned, as the story was getting suspenseful. The vampire fought a horde of demons with nothing but a dagger.

"It looks important," her mum yelled from downstairs.

Lilah sighed. Nothing was more important than finding out whether he'd free his soul from the demon king's claim or end up in Hell. But as long as her mother pestered her, she could not read in peace. "I'm coming."

She put the book on the bedside table, stretched, and trudged down the stairs.

Her mother waited in the corridor with a letter in her hands, tapping her right foot. "You're still in your pj's? It's past noon. You can't sleep all day!"

"I wasn't sleeping."

Her mum did not understand her fascination with fictional worlds, so she didn't mention she'd slept less than three hours, because the book enthralled her. She was the exact opposite of her mother in many ways. While her mum styled her short, platinum-blonde hair perfectly and only left the house dressed for eating at a five-star restaurant, Lilah didn't care for appearances. She didn't go out much, anyway.

"You've got mail from the university." Her mother

handed her the letter.

She opened it and started reading. *We are pleased to congratulate you on your admission to our bachelor's study program.*

"I got in," she said flatly.

Her mother's face lit up. "Congratulations, honey! I'm so proud of you."

"Thanks."

"Could you be any less enthusiastic? Lilah, this is fantastic news!"

Was it? Since the program had no admission restrictions apart from finishing high school, getting in was no tremendous feat. She had applied because she didn't know what else to do after graduation. Although spending more years on studying seemed dull, it beat deciding on a career right away.

Planning her future felt like choosing between pest and cholera, since she could not imagine ever finding a job she'd enjoy. Every path led to boredom and repeating the same routine every day. And for what? One among billions of people walking this earth...what could she possibly achieve? Everything seemed pointless.

"Why don't you invite a few friends and celebrate your success?"

She would have loved going for a drink or two with Amanda, a former classmate and friend, but Amanda had left the country. *Work and travel in Australia must be so much more exciting than staying at home and deciding on a study program.* She did not have the funds to join her friend. Besides, if she traveled to a place where many of the world's most dangerous animals lived, her mum would never let her hear the end of it.

She didn't consider any of her other classmates as

friends, and everyone else who qualified as fun to hang out with lived too far away.

"I'll pass." *I prefer reading anyway.*

"Well, suit yourself, honey. I'd invite you to a fancy dinner if I didn't already have a date tonight. Maybe we can go out tomorrow?"

"Sure, have fun tonight, Mum." She made her way up the stairs and sighed.

Another date? Hadn't her mum just broken up with someone? Ever since her father's death six years ago, her mother had dated one guy after the other. She yearned for someone by her side, no matter whom. Her self-indulgent lifestyle provided a sobering example of how Lilah did not want to live.

After taking a shower, she dived back into her book.

****

The sun had long set by the time Lilah finished reading. She turned on her PC. No news from Amanda, but a message from Julia popped up on her screen.

Hi, how are you? Have you finished the book yet?

Lilah smiled. Even though they'd never met in person, she loved chatting with Julia. Before she could answer, a loud crash from downstairs drew her attention.

"Mum?" she asked.

"Hello, honey…I'm ba-ack," her mother called.

"Are you all right?" She hurried downstairs to check. The coatrack lay knocked over on the floor, and her mum was trying to put it back up.

"Let me help you," she offered, but her mum pushed her away.

"Don't need your…your help. Whatcha doin' here, anyway? Go out and find…find yourself a cute boy, you know?" After fixing the coatrack, she stumbled toward her daughter.

Lilah caught her with a sigh. "You're drunk."

"I'm not drunk. Not drunk," her mother slurred. "I had this amazing evening with Thomas…No, wait, his name is…Timo. He's so-o handsome."

"Great. How about you go to bed now and tell me more about him tomorrow?" Dealing with Drunk Mum was never fun. She turned to leave, but her mother's next words stopped her in her tracks.

"You're not telling me when to go to bed! You…you jealous or what?"

Not again. She grimaced. "Mum, please go to bed."

"You're so-o jealous. I got all the cute boys and you…you sittin' alone at home."

"I don't need to date a hundred guys to be happy."

"But you do! Life's about finding…finding a perfect guy and…and a job. You wastin' your life away and…and you jealous I'm livin' mine."

Ouch! Drunk Mum was right. Not about being jealous or dating hundreds of guys, but…she was wasting her life, wasn't she? She'd lost her ambition when her father died. Seeing how little his achievements meant after his passing and how people gradually forgot about him devastated her. He hadn't wasted his life, though.

When her mother swayed dangerously on her way up the stairs, she tried to steady her, which ignited another rant. "Don't touch me! You think…think I need you? You tryin'…tryin' and tellin' me how to live my life. I'm drunk? I…I need to go to bed? How about…how about you first achieve…something before you lecture me?"

Even though she knew her mum didn't mean any of

it, she could not listen to another word. "I need some air." She pushed past her mother, grabbed her backpack from her room, put on running shoes, and stormed out.

Chapter 2

The crescent moon hung high in the dark sky as Lilah roamed the deserted streets of her neighborhood. Logic told her she shouldn't be out alone at this hour, but she didn't care. She'd always loved the mystery of the night. Even as a child, she slipped outside and gazed at the stars when she felt sad. They gave her hope that life offered more than what she knew. Besides, she needed to clear her head, and the fresh air on this warm summer night calmed her.

With worries about an uncertain future preoccupying her mind, she didn't pay attention to her surroundings until a shiver ran through her body. She didn't recognize the street she walked on, and her instincts told her she wasn't alone. Someone—or something—was lurking in the shadows, watching her every move.

It's not human. It was a silly thought or maybe wishful thinking. Most of the books, movies, and TV shows she devoured featured vampires and other things that go bump in the night. Meeting someone, or rather something, right out of her favorite works of fiction excited her.

Or maybe the prospect of something supernatural lying in wait comforted her more than the idea of a serial killer or rapist stalking her. Either way, she stopped to look around in hopes of finding a way out of a potentially dangerous situation.

Old-looking town houses lined the narrow, cobbled street. They were dark. Their inhabitants were asleep or not at home. The only light came from a single streetlamp behind her, about two meters from where she stood. Only her breathing interrupted the silence.

She took a few more steps before pausing again. Apart from her feet echoing on the cobblestones, there was no sound. Nothing hinted at anyone walking nearby, following her, or breathing in her vicinity. And yet, the goose bumps on her skin convinced her otherwise.

She preferred finding out about her pursuer sooner rather than later. As she couldn't achieve anything by staying quiet, she summoned up her courage to speak. "Stop hiding yourself. I know you're there...I can't see or hear you...But I can feel you watching me." With a whisper, she added the word "vampire."

A chuckle coming from behind her broke the silence. She squealed, and when she turned around, a tall, young man with shoulder-length, chocolate-brown hair, pale skin, and a long, dark leather coat was standing below the streetlight. He hadn't been there when she'd checked her surroundings earlier, and there had been no footsteps indicating anyone had walked up to her.

"Interesting," he said. "I didn't expect you to notice me. How did you recognize me for what I am without even seeing me?" He spoke softly, as if not to frighten her.

How indeed? She did not have a rational explanation.

"Call it a gut feeling or a verbalization of my deepest hopes." Her heartbeat thrummed in her ears. Was she actually talking to a vampire?

"Your deepest hopes? Why do I, a vampire, instill hope instead of fear in you?"

"I've prayed for something more than a mundane life. Meeting a vampire is not an everyday experience, so I'm thrilled." And possibly screwed, depending on what he wanted from her.

The vampire smiled, revealing his fangs. "Even if meeting me is the last experience you'll ever have? Aren't you afraid to die?"

She'd never contemplated her death. The possibility of her life ending in an instant stole her breath. But wasn't a short, exciting life worth much more than a long and boring existence? Didn't meeting with a vampire top everything she could hope for, in a world which often felt meaningless?

"I'm more afraid of living without ever feeling alive." Despite her words, her voice trembled.

"So you'll give me your blood and your life?"

"I don't mind donating some blood, but my life is a different matter. If it's up to me, I'd prefer to keep it." She gulped. Did she have a choice? "Death by vampire doesn't sound too bad, though. There are worse or more boring ways to die. And when you talk about taking my life, does it mean I'll die for good, or will your bite turn me into a vampire as well?"

He answered with a dry laugh. "I'm sorry to disappoint you, girl, but a simple bite won't turn you. We'd be out of food in no time if every human we bit became a vampire. No, we can choose to turn a human, but it's not a choice taken lightly. I won't condemn anyone to this miserable life."

"You've got a sad view of your life."

"You're one to talk. Your life doesn't seem to

fascinate you either."

"It didn't until today," she admitted. "You've shown me something fascinating. The existence of vampires and a world beyond the one I know as a human is giving me hope for a more interesting tomorrow."

The vampire vanished from where he stood, only to appear right behind her. "What a pity there won't be another tomorrow for you."

She flinched. She hadn't even seen or heard him move. When she turned around, he stood mere inches from her face. As he was a head taller than her, she had to look up to meet his piercing eyes. They held a sadness, which was uncanny for someone with such a youthful appearance. Did he feel sorry for having to take yet another life on his long, lonely journey?

Something in his eyes inspired her.

"You don't have to take my life tonight. Take me with you as your companion. I'm sure you could use some company?"

A sad smile formed on his face. "What a nice proposition, but I must decline. The road I follow is better walked alone."

She neither flinched nor resisted when the vampire took her in his arms, brushed her long, blonde hair aside, and tilted her head to prepare for his bite. Tremors shook her body when the implications hit her. She'd die, and there was no way to prevent it. Resisting him was futile and probably more painful than surrendering.

"I'd still advise against taking my life," she said.

"You would? Care to elaborate?"

She collected her thoughts for a last defense against death. She didn't want to give up on her life. Not now. "Well...How often do you get the chance to find a companion? You might regret not taking me up on my offer. Even if I'm only a walking bag of blood to you—what's the worst possible outcome? I can tell you're lonely and tired of your monotonous life. So am I."

"Save your breath," he said. "Although you're entertaining for a human, you don't fit into my world. Accept your fate." With these words, he tilted his head to bite her.

Moments before his fangs pierced her skin, she whispered, "Promise me one thing...never forget about me."

The vampire paused for an instant. "What?"

"As long as you remember me, my memory will live on for eternity. It's a comforting thought, isn't it?"

With a chuckle, he bit down on her neck. She gasped, but more out of surprise than pain. The bite didn't hurt. Instead, a warm, pleasurable feeling spread from the wound through her body. A moan escaped from her lips, and her knees buckled. Her grip on consciousness faded as his strong arms kept her from dropping to the ground.

Chapter 3

Lilah lay in an unfamiliar room on a single bed. It took her a second to piece the events of the previous night together. As soon as she remembered everything, an adrenaline rush hit her. She carefully felt her neck, expecting to find bite marks. Yet her skin was smooth, as if the vampire's fangs had never pierced it. Had their encounter been a dream? Was she still dreaming? She pinched herself, and it hurt. No dream, then. Where the hell was she, and what was she doing here?

Apart from the bed with white linen, there was a small wardrobe, a chair, and a bedside table with a candle, a box of matches, and a glass filled with water. The pieces of furniture were white and wooden, and a simple lamp hung from the ceiling. The sun shone through the only window.

She got up to look outside and found herself on the second floor of a big house made of stone, surrounded by trees and mountains covered with more trees in the background. Wherever she was, it wasn't close to home, since coastal areas and plains shaped the landscape near her hometown in northern Germany.

One wall held a white, ornate door. As she could not open it, she snooped around instead. The wardrobe turned out to be empty except for a backpack—her backpack. When she rummaged through her stuff, she noticed her smartphone was missing. Maybe it was for the best, since calling home to explain a vampire had kidnapped her would not ease her mother's worries about her absence. She could have used it to pinpoint her location, though.

Frustrated, she took a piece of gum out of her backpack and chewed it. She wasn't dead yet, which she took as a good sign. But why had he taken her to this strange place? She paced around, her emotions a mixture of worry and excitement for whatever awaited her. Eventually, she lay back down on the bed and tried to relax, with little success.

Time passed slowly while she listened for any sign of her captor coming to see her. Even after the sunset, nothing happened. Had he forgotten about her? Her stomach rolled. What if no one came for her? The growing darkness alarmed her even more, so she turned on the light. She'd almost expected the lamp not to work in such a remote place, but it did.

She started from a nap when the door swung open and the vampire entered. How much time had passed? She sat up on the bed as he closed the door behind him. He positioned himself on the chair, facing her. Her heart hammered as she took in his appearance in the room's light.

The long-sleeved shirt and the tight jeans he wore accentuated his muscular body. His flawless alabaster skin contrasted with his ocean-green eyes. Even though he held no smile on his thin lips, his soft facial features made his oval face seem gentle. *Beautiful.* She blushed as the thought entered her mind. This was not the time to drool over his looks. Was he waiting for her to speak?

"Why?" she asked after a few minutes of silent admiration.

"Why what? You need to specify your question."

"Why am I still alive?"

"Oh…" He sighed. "Contrary to popular belief, we don't have to kill the human we feed on. I only kill if I must, for example, if I face a hunter or encounter a human who knows too much. Although, technically, you fall into the second category."

"Why did you bring me…wherever we are?" Did he plan to kill her? She hugged her arms around her knees, and a shiver ran down her spine.

"Another why?" He chuckled. "Let's blame it on boredom. I got the impression you don't think you fit into your world. I thought I'd take you up on your offer and give you a chance to dive into mine if you're still up for it?"

"Well, you've just admitted you'd kill me if I wasn't up for it. So, you're not really giving me a choice here."

"To clarify, I have other options to handle a human knowing too much, especially if said human has only been aware of us for a short time. I can play tricks on your mind to make you believe everything has been a dream. Now, with no threat to your life to worry about, what would you decide?"

She met his eyes, trying to discern the truth in his words. Although he seemed innocent and gentle, he was a creature of the night. "Considering how powerful you are, you could keep me here regardless of what I want. So why do you care?"

"What do you think I am? A monster without a conscience?" Pain flickered across his face. He broke their gaze, stood up, and started pacing. "I might have brought you here out of boredom, but I'm not cruel. Living in my world isn't easy. It's dangerous and different from everything you've known.

"If you don't adapt, you'll get yourself killed and cause problems for me. So, keeping you here against your will is more trouble than it's worth. Once you agree to stay, you can never turn back. You can't contact anyone you knew, and you can never go back home. The risk is too big. Now, do you wish to stay or return to your old life?"

What would she return to? Friends who lived too far away, a somewhat misguided and sometimes overbearing mother, and years of studying at the local university? Leaving everything behind scared her, but…While she did not know what awaited her, anything beat returning to her mundane life. "I want to stay."

"Why?" the vampire asked with a grin.

"Why not…? Call it curiosity. I won't pass up the chance to see things most humans never will. There's nothing else out there for me, anyway. My family will miss me, but they've never understood me, and I could never relate to their way of life. I…I feel like I don't belong with them." She also wished to get to know him.

"Nothing to lose, eh? I can't promise you'll feel more at home in my world, but I'm curious how it'll turn out."

"So…" she said, "what does staying with you mean? What can I expect?"

The vampire laughed. "You agree to stay without knowing the details and get cold feet afterward? I admit I haven't thought it through myself. My world is dangerous, so there are a few basic rules.

"Staying means you *have* to trust me with your life. If I tell you to do something, I expect you to obey without question. You can trust I'll keep you from harm and protect you, but you must stay true to me in return." He waited for her to nod. "I might also drink your blood now and then, but as you've seen, it's usually not a painful experience."

Memories of his bite flooded her mind, and her cheeks heated. The experience had been far from painful, almost intimate.

His eyes wandered to her throat with a knowing smile, and he licked his lips. "Anything else you'd like to know?"

"Well, I've got plenty of questions. For now, how about telling me your name? I'm Lilah."

"Cain."

"Nice to meet you, Cain."

"All right, Lilah. Let me show you around."

Her new home wasn't just a house, but a small castle. There were two bathrooms and five more bedrooms—most of them fancier than hers—on the second floor. No one seemed to inhabit the other rooms. Cain suggested she move to another one, but she didn't want to. Hers offered everything she needed. One of the bathrooms was rather large with a big, fancy bathtub, two washbasins, and artfully decorated golden taps, which looked like the mouths of dragons.

The first floor comprised a study, a music room with a piano, and a cozy living room with a beige couch close to a small fireplace, a floor lamp, a side table, and a cuckoo clock. An impressive library offered many rare books in different languages. The smell of leather, glue, and thousands of words on decaying pages promised hours of quiet entertainment.

The ground floor had a gigantic living room with three leather couches, a coffee table, a billiard table, and—to her surprise—a small TV. Even though a layer of dust covered most of the appliances in the adjoining kitchen, as if no one cooked in there, various kinds of food filled the fridge. Did Cain eat at all? And if he didn't, had he bought these items in anticipation of her staying with him?

Pricey-looking pieces of art, most of them showing landscapes or people from the sixteenth century, hung on the walls of almost every room.

"This is off-limits," he declared when they came to a locked door blocking the way to the basement.

She tilted her head. Did it lead to a dungeon filled with captives or the place where he slept? Either way, she had no reason to go there. "All right."

He led her out of the house, which looked like a square, two-story castle keep with large windows and a flat roof. There was nothing except for fir trees. Not even a path led to his home. "I'd advise you against straying far from the house since there is nothing—no street, no building, no living person—around here for miles. If you get lost in these woods, chances are you won't get out alive."

She frowned. "How did we get here?"

"Teleportation. I'm capable of transporting me and anything or anybody I touch to any place I've visited. A remote home offers certain advantages."

She pursed her lips. If he was telling the truth, she could never change her mind about leaving, because there was nowhere to go.

"So, I guess you've seen everything." He handed her a key. "Make yourself at home because this is your home now."

"Thanks."

"Apart from the basement, you can move around the entire house, use the appliances, and do as you like. I know you still require clothes and things, but I have other obligations to attend to tonight. I'll try to take you shopping tomorrow."

"Can't I join you wherever you're going tonight?"

Instead of answering, he shook his head and vanished.

She groaned. Why did he leave her behind? She locked the front door on her way inside and then settled on eating snacks while watching TV. All local channels broadcast in a language she did not recognize. Was she in a foreign country? After several hours of listening to a music TV show, she fell asleep on the couch.

When the warm sun on her face woke her around noon, someone—probably Cain—had turned off the TV and covered her with a blanket. Disappointment welled up in her because he hadn't woken her upon his return. As a vampire, he probably slept during the day. With a few hours to kill before sunset, she went to sleep in her room to attune her sleeping rhythm to Cain's.

Chapter 4

When Lilah woke up, Cain was sitting on the chair, watching her. Only the glow of the moon allowed her to discern the vampire's silhouette.

"You know that's creepy, right?" she asked.

"Sorry." He laughed and hit a switch. She only realized he'd moved when the light blinded her. "I didn't want to wake you, but since we don't have all night, I thought we should get going soon."

"You wanted to take me shopping, right? How? It's dark outside, so it must be late. Where will we find an open store?"

"Everything here's already closed," he agreed, "but I never said we'd be shopping nearby. I propose we skip two or three time zones. In some countries, shopping centers stay open until at least ten p.m., which gives us enough time."

"We're skipping time zones?" She gaped at him.

He chuckled. "You might not have realized it, but we've already skipped some coming here. As I said, I can teleport to most places I've visited. The distance doesn't matter as long as I can picture the location."

"Isn't the sun still up where we're going?"

"Yes, but it won't kill me, if that's what you're worried about. We avoid the sun because it weakens us. Our eyes are sensitive to light, which can be a disadvantage in a fight. However, to a powerful vampire, sunlight doesn't cause more than a mild allergic reaction. Since it drains our energy, younger vampires can't do anything but sleep all day. I'm not young, though. I suggest you trust I know what I'm doing and join me on a quick trip."

"Fair enough. Give me two minutes to get ready." She disappeared into the enormous bathroom to freshen up.

Once she was finished, she found Cain skimming through a book in the library. When she approached, he put it back on a shelf and spread his arms as if inviting her for a hug.

She eyed him skeptically.

"Come here. I don't bite." He chuckled.

"Really?" She raised her eyebrows.

"At least not tonight."

With hesitant steps, she went into his arms. He put his left hand on the back of her head and his right on her waist to hold her close. Her heart fluttered when she inhaled his masculine, woodsy scent.

"Close your eyes for a moment," he said, and she obeyed.

Her skin tingled, and her stomach churned as if riding a roller coaster. The sensation lasted for less than two seconds. When she opened her eyes, they were in a small alley. Ocher and terra-cotta hues colored most of the houses, and pine trees decorated the gardens.

"Welcome to Spain," he said.

She stared at him with an open mouth.

"You'll get used to it." He grinned. "Come on."

They walked two blocks to a big shopping center. In less than an hour, she found shoes, pants, shirts, sweatshirts, pajamas, and a coat. Most of the items were black and more comfortable than stylish.

"Did you get everything you need?" he asked.

"Not exactly…" Despite three full bags of clothes, she lacked underpants and bras, but she dreaded buying those with Cain around. When he eyed her expectantly, she added, "I still need underwear."

"Oh." His gaze darted around the shopping center. "There's a store right around the corner. Why don't you go ahead and buy what you need, and I'll meet you in a little while?" He handed her a two-hundred-euro bill.

"Thanks!" She accepted his money with wide eyes and made her way to the store. When she left it half an hour later with a new bag, he was waiting in front of its entrance.

"I'm done now." She smiled at him.

"You finished shopping much faster than I expected, considering I offered to buy whatever you fancied."

She shrugged. "I don't care about fashion."

"Since it's still early, how about getting something to eat? Do you like Spanish food?"

Spanish food in Spain? What a treat! She nodded. "Do you?"

"I don't eat."

Lilah silently berated herself for not figuring it out herself.

"How about you choose a nearby restaurant, and while you eat, I'll answer any questions you might have regarding vampires? It's best to get those out of the way early on so you know what you're dealing with."

"Sounds great! I've got tons of questions." A wide grin formed on her face.

Ten minutes later, they seized two chairs in front of a tiny restaurant in a back alley. There were only two tables outside, and an older married couple occupied the other.

After ordering their drinks, Cain surveyed the surrounding area. "I don't think anyone's paying attention to us. Ask away."

"Let's start with the common rumors. You told me about your reaction to sunlight, but what about other myths like immortality, garlic, and wooden stakes?"

"The cliches, eh? I guess some truth lies in most of them. We are immortal, if that's what you call not aging and never getting sick. Vampires can die, though. Young and weak vampires die more easily than experienced, powerful ones. Wooden stakes are useless—something as fragile as wood cannot hurt us."

His gaze focused on the waiter who headed for their table. "And with our heightened senses, the smell of garlic might be unpleasant, but it won't keep us away. So order anything you like."

The waiter placed their drinks on the table and asked for her order. When he turned to Cain, the vampire told him he wasn't hungry.

After the waiter left, she eyed Cain's glass. "You told me you don't eat, but what about drinking? Can you drink?"

As a response, he took a sip of his wine. "I can, but it's more of a social thing. I don't require water, and I couldn't get drunk if I wanted. It's still fun to pretend sometimes."

Her eyes fell on the cutlery on their table. "Does silver affect you?"

"It does. Just like the sun, silver feels uncomfortable and weakens us, but it doesn't necessarily kill us. If you were to attack a vampire, silver would be your choice of weapon. Other weapons hurt us, but we heal too fast for it to matter, whereas silver-coated ones slow the healing process.

"If you ram a silver-coated stake into a vampire's heart or shoot us with a silver bullet—depending on the exact spot and the vampire's age, experience, and power—it can be fatal. Decapitation kills us, too. Nothing can survive without a head. Fire or being burned alive hurts, although we can heal from burns with no lasting effects as long as we're not reduced to ashes by the flames."

"Why are you telling me about all the ways I can kill you?"

"Don't assume you could kill me—you're far too weak. Nonetheless, knowing how to defend yourself in this world could save your life."

She gulped. "I hope I won't have to resort to this knowledge."

"Silver is also useful for keeping a vampire contained. Because of its weakening properties, it's one of the few materials we can't destroy by brute force."

"What about mirrors?"

He shrugged. "I don't know where rumors about mirrors come from. My guess is, after living for hundreds of years, some vampires don't care for their reflection anymore. But not caring doesn't make them invisible. The same goes for the similar rumor regarding pictures. And yet, vampires almost never appear in them.

"Because of our longevity, we can't afford for humans to recognize us in a hundred-year-old photo. So, any rationally thinking vampire will avoid being photographed. With the rise of smartphones and social media, staying anonymous is getting harder, though."

"Do you possess any supernatural abilities apart from teleportation?"

Her order—a variety of tapas—arrived.

He paused long enough for the waiter to disappear before he answered, "We're stronger, faster, and more durable than any human. Our heightened senses make us better predators, and we've got an additional sense telling us if other vampires are nearby and how strong they are."

"How does that work?" she asked between bites.

"Every vampire has a specific aura which differs from a human's. Many powerful vampires manipulate theirs to conceal their true strength, but only a few can hide their otherness. Vampires recognize one another by their aura." He studied her. "Humans with a weak variant of this skill are rare but not unheard of. I wonder if you subconsciously noticed my aura when you spotted me two days ago."

"I don't know. Maybe it was luck?"

"Luck? I don't think luck had anything to do with it. Your instincts warned you."

She grinned. "Well, I obviously didn't heed the warning."

"No, you really didn't." His lips parted and revealed his fangs. Her breath caught when their eyes met, the intensity of his gaze reminding her of the heat she'd felt from his bite. After a long moment, he cleared his throat.

"Regarding a vampire's abilities…apart from the basics, everything depends on power and experience. Teleportation is merely one example. Some vampires possess telekinetic or telepathic skills, like reading minds or controlling people."

"Do you?"

"Why, are you wondering what your thoughts reveal about you?" His gaze fixated on her forehead for a moment before his expression turned into a teasing grin. "Don't worry, I can't read minds…At least not the way you'd imagine. But I can read intentions, so I know if someone is lying, for example. Or are you worried about me controlling you?"

She shook her head. *Somehow, I don't think he would…*

"It's nothing I've ever tried and nothing I'd ever want to. I hate the idea of taking someone's will. Controlling someone would only control their body and not their thoughts. They'd be aware of being forced to do something they don't want, without being able to stop it." He grimaced, disgusted.

"A horrible notion." She shivered. "What else can you do?"

"We possess certain abilities in connection to drinking blood." He licked his lips. "Blood is what we live on. We need to feed regularly, although the interval depends on a vampire's age. For me, once every three to five days is sufficient. While feeding, we can inject our donors with fluids which have various effects. With these fluids, we can erase the pain or make the bite pleasurable. We can make our donors sleepy or lose consciousness. We can also poison them, immobilize them, or tamper with their short-term memories."

"These abilities are quite convenient to prevent the world from finding out about you." She put her knife and fork on her empty plate.

"They definitely are. If you're satisfied, I'll bring you back home so you can unpack your new stuff."

He paid the waiter and led her to an empty alley from where he teleported them to his house. To her disappointment, he left again right away without her.

Chapter 5

When Lilah went downstairs to make herself breakfast early the next evening, Cain was reading a book in the living room.

"What were you doing last night?" she asked.

He looked up for a second before he focused on his book again. "Working."

"What does a vampire do for work?"

"It depends…Not every vampire works. Since we don't need to pay for food or other utilities, we can get by with little money. Many vampires invest, though. We live for a long time, and antiques, shares, and property become more and more valuable with every decade."

"So…you're an investor?"

"No."

"Then what is it you do for a living?" Did she have to drag every word out of him?

He put the book aside with a sigh. "For the lack of a better term, I'm a mercenary. I take care of hunters who pose a danger to our kind, or rogue vampires who threaten to expose us."

"Sounds exciting."

" 'Exciting' isn't the word I'd use. It's brutal and dangerous, and it involves killing. I don't enjoy taking lives, but it's necessary, and…I'm good at it," he said with a devilish smile.

A chill traveled down her spine. "Were you hunting

the past two nights?"

He nodded.

Was he truly a murderer? He was a vampire, and they were in his world, with different rules, so Lilah did not presume to judge him. She aspired to understand this part of his life, though. "Why don't you take me along next time?"

"Did you get the part where I kill people?"

She swallowed hard. "I know what I signed up for when I stayed, so I don't mind…"

"My assignments are often too risky for you to tag along."

"I'll be careful. Come on, you can't leave me at home all day long."

He pondered her words for a moment. "You have a point…Or I haven't thought this through. As long as I'm going after humans, there is no harm in taking you along. They'll believe you're just another one of my victims, so they won't go after you. However, I expect you to be on alert the entire time and to listen to whatever I tell you to do, the second I tell you to do it. You need to play your part as well."

****

"What are we after?" Lilah asked Cain a few hours later. They strolled down a deserted street leading out of a small village, with woods on one side of the street and remote farms on the other. The stink of cow dung hung strong in the air.

He'd taken a long sword and two daggers on this mission and provided her with one of the daggers to defend herself. They concealed their weapons beneath their clothes. Both of them wore long, black coats.

"*I'm* going after a group of hunters," he emphasized.

"Several vampires reported seeing them a month ago. Since I could locate none of these vampires for follow-up questions, chances are the hunters killed them."

"Kill or die," she said.

"That's what this world is about. Is it exciting enough for you yet? By the way, we're being followed."

Adrenaline rushed into her body. She halted to look for their pursuers, but he gently pushed her along.

"I noticed them a while ago, but I don't want them to know I'm aware of their presence. I'm still waiting for their backup to arrive. Keep walking and pretend you're having a good time," he whispered into her ear.

"I don't have to pretend."

Twigs snapped up ahead, and two men, one of them equipped with a broadsword and the other one with a gun, appeared out of the forest five meters from her and Cain's location. Feet shuffled on the ground behind her, betraying the approach of two more hunters, and another pair ran toward them from a farmhouse on the left side of the street.

"You're surrounded," the man with the broadsword said. "Slowly raise your hands, step away from the girl, and surrender."

Cain laughed. "Have you watched too many crime shows?"

He grabbed Lilah and pulled her in front of him like a shield while turning so the trees were at his back.

"What?" she exclaimed.

"Get away from her!" a female hunter to their left shouted.

"Or what?" Cain asked. "You don't want to hurt her. As long as she's here, you won't assault me. I'd also advise you not to attack at all."

"Why? Do you think you scare us? It's six against one, so you better surrender," another female hunter with short, chestnut-blonde hair yelled. She aimed her gun at him from across the street, standing in front of a large estate surrounded by a knee-high hedge.

"Numbers aren't everything when you're up against a vampire," Cain answered.

"If you're so sure of yourself, release her and face us."

"And let my meal go? Fighting with an empty stomach is no fun. Besides, if you come at me as soon as I let her go, I can just as well kill her."

"Kill me?" Lilah asked in a shrill voice. He wanted her to play an unsuspecting victim, so she did. Although, if she were an unsuspecting victim, he'd only make her fall unconscious and alter her memories.

The hunter with the broadsword who stood on Lilah's right side smiled at her with rotten teeth. "Don't worry, sweetie, we'll save you from this monster."

Ugh. Don't call me sweetie. I don't even want you to save me.

Cain snorted. "How do you plan to save her? Don't make promises you can't keep. As of now, you can't attack me without injuring her."

The hunters whispered among themselves. She couldn't make out their conversation, but Cain could. "You don't have to trade her freedom for my life," he said. "It's not my life you should worry about. And I don't need safe passage from you."

"You cocky bastard! Just wait till we bring you down," another male hunter yelled.

Cain laughed. "I am waiting, and nothing's happening. I'm getting bored here, so I'll have my dinner now."

He ignored the angry cries of the hunters, pushed her head to one side, and bit down on her neck.

She gasped for breath when a wave of pleasure hit her. "Pretend to faint, and drop to the ground," his voice echoed in her head. When he released her—far too soon for her liking—she swayed, sank to her knees, and fell to her right side. Her long hair spread across her face, allowing her to peek through the strands with no one noticing she was fine.

Seeing her drop triggered something in the hunters. They stormed toward Cain as he drew his sword.

From her spot on the gravel ground, she only saw glimpses of their fight, but she didn't dare move. Cain evaded three bullets fired from different directions and blocked the attacks of three hunters, who came rushing at him one after another, before he vanished from her field of vision.

Someone screamed. Another gunshot echoed through the night. Metal clashed against metal, followed by the sound of something heavy hitting the ground.

"Look out!" a female voice shrieked, and Lilah winced.

A gunshot thundered nearby, followed by a gurgling sound and the thumps of two bodies falling down.

"Save yourself! I'll keep him occupied," one of the male hunters shouted.

The chestnut blonde rejected his offer. "I won't leave you behind. We'll get him together!"

When their voices were no longer in her vicinity, Lilah turned her head to watch the battle. Only two hunters—the chestnut blonde and a tall male with black hair, fighting Cain with a sword—remained. Since they moved a lot, the female hunter couldn't risk firing her weapon, instead she stared at their duel in horror. Her gun was useless in her hands.

The male hunter tried hard to fend Cain off, but his skills were lacking, and Cain pushed him farther back with each slash. Not paying attention to his surroundings, the hunter stumbled over the hedge. Cain used the hunter's clumsiness to his advantage, although he didn't need to. With one blow, he severed the man's hand, and his head with the next strike of his sword.

"You're a monster!" the female hunter shouted and fired her gun. The shot didn't hit Cain, as he vanished. A few seconds later, she cried out in pain when he buried his fangs into her neck. Her body became limp, and she dropped to the floor.

In less than five minutes, he'd reduced the group of hunters to a pitiful pile of bodies. After checking his surroundings, he walked over to Lilah. "Are you okay?"

She put herself in a sitting position. Her body shivered, and she avoided looking at his face. Even though she knew what she'd gotten herself into, the sight shocked and terrified her.

"I will be," she mumbled.

"Give me a moment to clean this mess up." He sighed, picked up two bodies, and disappeared. A minute later, he reappeared without them and repeated the process twice until he'd destroyed most evidence of his deed. The next rain would wash away the rest.

He squatted down, coming face-to-face with her. "Mind if I heal your puncture wounds?"

She touched her neck and stared at her bloody fingers. She hadn't even realized she was bleeding from his bite. "Go ahead." Her voice held no vigor.

He pricked his finger on one of his teeth. When he smeared his blood on her wounds, they healed.

"Thanks," she said weakly.

"You look pale. Let me take you home for now."

She flinched when he reached for her hand and instantly regretted her reaction.

His expression fell and his shoulders dropped for a moment before he hid his emotions behind a mask of nonchalance. "So...Seeing me kill is too much for you."

"No, I..." Was it too much? It was a lot to take in, but the hunters sealed their fate by going after vampires. She shook her head. "I didn't mean to react badly, sorry...I needed a moment to process everything. These hunters attacked us. No one can blame you for taking them down."

"I did not kill them because they attacked us. It's my job to bring death to humans. Death is what I am. Death is what every human fears." His expression darkened.

She shook her head again, a sad smile forming on her lips. "I'm not afraid of you, and I never will be. You're not death. You're doing what's necessary to survive, so don't think so lowly of yourself."

"Why not? After all, I robbed the hunters of their lives."

She could not deny that. But unlike the drunk bastard who'd run over her father with his car and left him for dead, Cain took their lives for a valid reason.

"You're not a villain. You killed them so they wouldn't kill you or any other vampire, didn't you?"

He nodded.

"Don't paint yourself as a monster because you have to take lives. A veritable monster does not regret its deeds," she said.

His eyes widened slightly. He didn't refute her bold claim.

****

The sight of lifeless bodies stayed on her mind for hours after their return, but a beautiful melody drew her from grim memories. She followed it to find Cain playing a piece on the piano. As she didn't wish to disturb him, she stayed in the doorway and listened quietly. Even though she could not put a name to the melody, it was a well-known arrangement. She'd heard it before, years ago, back when her childhood friend used to play for her. She'd spent hours listening to him every day after school until he'd moved away. How long had it been since then? Four or five years? The music stopped.

"You look sad," Cain noted.

"I'm simply a little nostalgic," she answered. "Please don't cease playing on my behalf."

"How about I play something for you?"

A wide smile spread across her face. "I'd love that."

He returned her smile and gestured for her to join him on the piano bench. "What would you like me to play?"

Her heart rate quickened when she sat next to him and her arm brushed his. "Anything is fine."

When his fingers danced on the keys, she closed her eyes and let the music sweep her away.

Chapter 6

Dry leaves crunched beneath her feet, and a woodpecker hammered in the distance as Lilah wandered through the thick forest. Heavy fog hung in the air and restricted her vision.

The whooshing of water drew her to a nearby river, where she sought to moisten her dry throat. But its water shimmered blood-red, and she froze at the sight.

A wailing cry tore through the mist and made her shudder. What was going on? She followed the weeping, which became more desperate with every step she took.

A woman was bent over a lifeless body. Something about her seemed very familiar.

"Mum?" Lilah asked, but her mum didn't react. She approached the body to find out why her mother was grieving. It was the corpse of a young woman with long, caramel-blonde hair. A scream got stuck in her throat when she saw the pale face. She was staring at herself.

She woke in a cold sweat, shivering. *What a horrible dream!*

As falling back to sleep was out of the question, she got up, picked a change of clothes, and went into the bathroom. Although the warm water of the shower dripping down her skin soothed her, thoughts swirled through her mind. Was the nightmare a reflection on the previous night's carnage, or did it hold a deeper meaning? How was her mother coping without her?

After washing her worries away with berry-scented shower gel and coconut shampoo, she dried off, wrapped her wet hair in a towel, and got dressed. The bathroom clock showed three p.m.—the perfect time to pay a visit to the library. The first volume of an epic fantasy series caught her eye, so she read it in the cozy living room.

****

"You're up early." Cain's words drew her from the book a few hours later. He leaned against the doorway, wearing a black turtleneck and a black pair of jeans.

"I couldn't sleep," she said.

"Why?" He tilted his head. "Are you okay?"

"I…I had a bad dream. Nothing to worry about."

"Are you sure?" A look of concern passed over his face.

She forced a smile. "Yes, I'm fine."

"Let me know if you need anything."

"Actually…" She put the book down and met his eyes. *No harm in asking, right? Worst-case scenario, he says no.* "Could I write a short letter or something to my mother…to let her know I'm fine? I know you don't want me to contact anyone I know, but…I don't want her to worry."

He opened his mouth, struggling for words. "It's not about…wanting you to cut all ties to the human world. It's a necessary precaution so humans won't find out about us."

Oh. Her shoulders slumped. "What if…what if I don't reveal where I am or who I'm with? I simply long to say goodbye to help her move on. We can't have her searching the whole world for me…"

"Okay."

"Really?" Disbelief colored her voice.

"Yes, really." His warm smile reassured her. "I think it'll help you leave your old life behind. You can find a pen and paper in the study. I'll deliver the letter for you when you're done."

"Thanks!"

She made her way into the study, where she found a nice fountain pen and parchment paper. She sat down at the desk to write, but she struggled to find the right words. No matter what she wrote, it'd never be enough for her mother. But a brief note was still better than disappearing without a goodbye.

Dear Mum,

I'm sorry for not coming home. I left because I yearn for a different life. And I found what I was looking for, so please don't worry about me. I'm fine, but I won't return.

Even if we won't see each other again, I need you to know I'll always love you, and I'm thankful for everything you've done for me. Please take good care of yourself.

Love,

Lilah

After rereading her writing, she folded the parchment and put it in an envelope.

She found Cain in the downstairs living room. "I'm done. You wanna read it?"

He shook his head. "I'm sure it's fine. Do you want me to deliver it right now?"

"Yes, please." She handed him the letter. "Do you want me to write my address down?"

"No, I know where you used to live."

"How?" She frowned, as they hadn't discussed her background.

"Since I can't let just anyone into my life, I checked your bag before bringing you here," he admitted. "I glimpsed your address on your ID."

"Oh. Well, I'm glad I passed your examination."

"Me too." His sensuous smile made her heart leap. "I'll take care of your letter and some other business now, but I won't be long. See you in a bit."

After his departure, she ate a bowl of cereal and returned to the cozy living room to continue reading.

Shortly after the cuckoo clock struck midnight, he returned with a large pizza box and placed it on the side table. "I thought you might be hungry."

"Always." She peeked inside the box, and her mouth watered. Pepperoni on one half and tuna on the other— her favorite. "What a perfect combination! Too bad you can't have any."

"I'll be okay." He smiled as she bit into the first slice. "Mind if I join you?"

"Not at all," she said with a full mouth.

"Great." He fetched a book from the library and draped himself over the other half of the couch.

His proximity caused her stomach to flutter, so she gave up eating after three slices and focused on the book instead. When she stretched to get into a more comfortable position, her feet landed on his lap. She blushed and shot him an inquiring look. Did he mind? When he glanced at her with a smile, she relaxed.

They spent the rest of the night buried in their books. Even though she often read through the night, doing so right next to Cain was a whole new experience. Not because he was a vampire. His body did not feel any different from a human's. Having someone to share these moments with was an incredibly pleasant change. Had he been as lonely as her?

****

"How did you sleep?" Cain's voice surprised Lilah as she prepared her breakfast.

"Much better." She smiled at him while cutting a slice of bread. "What are you doing tonight?"

He shrugged before propping himself on the kitchen table, facing her.

"Will you go hunting?" she asked as she twirled the knife between her fingers on her way to the sink.

He raised an eyebrow at her. "Not tonight, no. I'm still waiting for a new assignment."

"Will you take me along again once you get one?"

His eyes widened. "Do you *want* to come along again?"

"Yes." She smiled softly at him before turning her attention to the fridge. "I'm sure having some company will make your assignments less dreary. Everything becomes more bearable when you don't have to face it alone."

"You don't have to join me for my sake, you know?" His expression softened as she turned to him with a pack of cheese in her hand. "I've been hunting on my own for a long time."

"I know, but I want to." She'd said goodbye to her old life. Staying by his side meant embracing the good and the bad.

"Okay…As long as the target's human, you can tag along. But don't force yourself." His lips tightened, and he tapped his fingers on the table.

"I won't." She put two slices of cheese on her bread and returned the rest to the fridge.

"A large part of hunting is exploring the area, so we

might even have some fun visiting different cities. Speaking of fun, what would you like to do today?" he asked.

"Well...What do you usually do for fun?"

"When I'm not out hunting, I spend most of my time here, working on my weapon skills, reading, or playing the piano."

His hobbies sounded no more social than most of hers. Time to add a few more activities to his list. "What about games?" she asked. "Do you like card or board games?"

"Games, eh? I've played a few, but nothing stuck."

"Want me to teach you some?" She scanned the room for something to play with. Her eyes passed the billiard table and an antique chessboard, but she yearned for something else. "Have you got a deck of cards?"

"Probably somewhere. Why don't you eat your breakfast while I track it down?"

An hour later, they faced each other from opposite sides of the coffee table. With a grin, Lilah played her next card. "Mau Mau."

"Another jack as your last card?" Cain sighed as he drew a card from the pile. "You're too good at this."

"I plan ahead with the cards I got." She put her jack of spades on the table. "Are you up for another round?"

"Sure. What do you say to raising the stakes?" He shot her a flirty gaze, and her stomach fluttered in response.

"What do you have in mind?" she asked with a hint of flirtation in her own voice.

"How about the winner gets your blood?" he said in a throaty voice.

She gulped. "My *blood*?" Her pulse quickened. She

secretly longed to experience the heat of his bite again, but then she'd have to lose. "Not a very enticing bet, since I can't gain anything." She rolled her eyes and picked up the remnants of their game.

"Oh, would you rather I bite you if you won?" he asked with a mischievous glint.

"I didn't say that." Her cheeks burned. Could he read her mind—expose her secret desire—after all?

He chuckled. "Let's just play. *If* you win, you can decide on your prize after the game."

"All right." She gathered the cards up and shuffled them. Her hands trembled when she dealt him his hand and revealed the queen of hearts as the first card from the deck.

He started his round with an eight of hearts, forcing her to skip her first turn.

She raised an eyebrow. "Did your competitiveness rise with the stakes?"

"I hope you're not backing down now?" He grinned, showing his fangs.

"Definitely not! I like challenges."

After several turns, he played a seven of diamonds. "Mau."

She gaped at him as she drew two cards. They offered no way to turn the tide.

He placed his last card, a queen of diamonds, on the table. "I win." His eyes met hers as he licked his lips. "Time for my prize. Come here."

She swallowed hard. Unlike the last two times, this situation felt more intimate. *No backing out now.* With trembling knees, she made her way over to him. Once she was within reach, he pulled her onto his lap. She sucked in a breath when her back nestled against his chest.

"Nothing to fear." The warmth of his breath tingled on her skin, and his voice sent a shiver of pleasure through her body. He brushed her hair aside and inhaled her scent. "Relax, okay?"

"Mhm."

He sank his teeth into her neck. After the briefest flicker of pain, an incredible heat spread from the bite through her body, followed by tingling. A moan escaped her as her mind went blank. Her muscles relaxed, and she became limp in his arms.

When she regained her senses, she was lying on the couch, her head on his lap.

"You okay?"

She sat up and blinked. "Yes…Just a little light-headed, I guess."

"Drink something." He handed her a glass of orange juice.

After taking a sip, she asked, "Does drinking blood feel just as good for you?"

"Better." He grimaced for a moment—or did she imagine it? "For a vampire, nothing compares to feeding on a human. But while my body thrives on blood, yours can't handle losing too much. So we should lower the stakes for our next game."

"All right." She smiled as she picked up the cards. "Do you know gin rummy?"

Chapter 7

Several weeks later, Lilah stayed home alone while Cain hunted a rogue vampire. She was reading an old Shakespearean book in the cozy living room when a loud thump from the ground floor caught her attention.

"Cain?" she asked.

No answer, just a muted groan from below brought her to hurry down to investigate. Cain was writhing on the living room floor, his clothes soaked in blood. Her heartbeat faltered as she ran the last few steps to him.

"Stay away!" he shouted before she reached him.

Startled by his outburst, she stopped in her tracks. "Are you all right? What happened?"

"Go away," he groaned.

One of his arms was in shreds, and blood gushed from his abdomen.

Even though her stomach turned from the sight, she edged closer. "I don't think leaving you right now is a good idea. You need help."

He gritted his teeth. "You can't help me. I crave blood."

"You can have mine."

"No! I can't guarantee your safety right now. I can barely stay awake, let alone control my hunger."

"Well, I'm offering, so where's the problem?" She frowned. He had fed on her countless times.

"Please leave. You don't know what you're

offering." He grimaced and writhed in front of her. "I'm not in control of my emotions. So I can't protect you from the pain. Stay away!" His breaths were shallow and labored.

She inhaled deeply. How could she leave if he was suffering? Her blood could ease the pain. "It takes less time for you to heal if you feed, doesn't it? I trust you. Take my blood. I can handle some pain."

"It's more than some pain. I might even kill you."

She swallowed hard, but his warning didn't change her resolve. "You told me the risk, and I'm willing to take it. Let me help you."

Kneeling down at his side, she offered her neck.

"If you insist, fine. But I won't drink from your neck." With his intact hand, he brought her left arm close to his mouth. His eyes met hers.

"Are you sure?" he asked in a shaky voice.

When she nodded, he bit into her wrist.

She expected the pangs of his sharp teeth piercing her skin, but not the sensation of him sucking the blood out of her. Each gulp tore at her insides, and her body convulsed. She tried to stifle her cry of pain without success.

He did not react to her whimpering. Even when her limbs tingled from the loss of blood, he kept drinking.

"Stop," she pleaded.

A guttural sound escaped him as he tore even deeper into her flesh. Had offering her blood been a stupid mistake?

Her heart thrashed in her chest, trying to keep the blood flowing. But for how long? She needed to bring him to his senses. "Look at me!"

But his ravenous eyes did not see her.

"Cain, stop!" Tears streamed down her face.

Her body became weaker and colder by the second. With the last of her strength, she tried to pull her wrist from his mouth, but he didn't budge. Darkness took away the pain.

****

Darkness greeted Lilah when she woke. Blinds in front of the window made deducing the time impossible. Her heart jumped when she rolled over to find Cain's face right next to hers. He'd fallen asleep hunched over, with his head resting on her bed. The wounds on his body had healed, and he wore fresh clothes. A wave of relief flooded her. With a smile, she wiped a strand of soft, chocolate-colored hair out of his face. She quickly withdrew her hand when he stirred.

"Hello." He smiled at her while stretching his muscles. "I'm glad you're awake. How are you?"

"Dizzy," she answered. "What happened?"

"Let me get you something to eat and drink first. You've lost too much blood." Without awaiting a reply, he vanished for a minute and returned with a glass of water and a sandwich.

"Thank you." She took a big bite of the ham and cheese.

"You know I've been hunting a rogue vampire. Even though I'd tailed him for a while, I hadn't met him face-to-face until last night."

"What turned him into a rogue?"

"Living for too long…He got bored and tried to spice up his life by exposing us and starting a war with humans. What a fool. Since we can't risk the entire world finding out about us, I set out to deal with him."

"Judging by your injuries, dealing with him wasn't

easy, was it?" She gulped.

"No, it wasn't. I knew I faced a tremendous foe because he was older than me, and with age comes power. Thanks to my fighting experience, I got the upper hand. But I lost a lot of blood, so it was hard for me to stay focused."

"What do you mean?"

"Our urges control us, and every vampire has the urge to drink blood and to kill. It takes practice and willpower to resist. When I'm not focused, I'm not in control, and it's not safe for you to be around me. Offering your blood to me sped up my healing process, but it put you at risk.

"If I'd taken a little more, you wouldn't have survived. I won't die from injuries like the ones from last night. You might die if I lose control." He shuddered. "So do me a favor and listen to me if we're ever in a similar situation. Don't risk your life for me."

She swallowed the last bite of her sandwich and crossed her arms. "It's still my life I'm risking! I won't hesitate if I can ease your suffering."

He smiled at her. "I appreciate it. But it's essential for you to heed my words if you wish to survive in this world. I don't want to take your life in a blood craze. After all, I promised to keep you from harm, and I intend to keep my promise. Don't make it unnecessarily tough for me by tempting fate."

"I get your point. Yet I can't suppress my desire to help you when you're in pain. I can't guarantee I won't do the same again in a similar situation."

He wasn't happy with her answer, but it was the best he'd get.

Chapter 8

In October, Lilah accompanied Cain on an assignment to Paris. Her eyes were glued to the display windows as they walked along a fancy street lined by baroque-style houses with little cafés and shops. "Those pastries look delicious! Can we come back another day during the opening hours?"

"We're not here to eat." He didn't even wait for her.

"Well, obviously you're not." She pouted as she ran after him to catch up. "Or how about paying a visit to the Eiffel Tower? I've always wanted to see it."

"No."

"Why not?" He usually indulged her.

He shrugged.

She narrowed her eyes at him. "What's wrong?"

"Nothing."

"Then why are you so snippy?"

"I'm not."

Really? She rolled her eyes. Somehow, she needed to get him to talk. "What are we looking for tonight?"

"Another vampire reported a small group of hunters around here. From what I've heard, they haven't ambushed anyone yet. They wouldn't do much damage either way, since Paris is the home of a powerful vampire who doesn't tolerate others. He could take care of these hunters himself, but…he doesn't fancy getting his hands dirty, which is why we're here."

"Sounds like a great guy," she said sarcastically.

He smiled wryly. "If I could afford to reject his assignment, I would, but he's quite influential, and being on his bad side is too much trouble."

"So…you don't mind the city but the person associated with it," she concluded.

"Let's just get this over with."

After a while, blocks of shabby apartment buildings replaced the baroque-style houses. Scattered trash, cigarette butts, and the stink of urine caused her to rethink her desire to explore the city.

When Cain jerked to a stop, she almost ran into him.

"Hide!" he hissed at her.

The urgency in his voice led her to react instantly. To her right, garbage containers filled a dead-end street. While their smell was unpleasant, their size hid her from sight, so she cowered behind one of them. Her heart thundered in her ears as she peeked through a slit between the container and the adjacent wall.

Cain's footsteps echoed off the pavement as he walked away from her. Was he deliberately making noises?

A chilly breeze blew through the street, and a dark figure appeared. Cain kneeled before the slim, short man with light hair. Something about him made her hair stand on end. Because of the distance, she only heard fragments of their conversation.

"I see you've taken on my assignment. I expected you to check in with me before coming here, but so be it. How's your progress?" the stranger asked. While he had an arrogant and commanding voice, Cain spoke in a quiet, subservient tone.

Lilah didn't understand Cain's reply, but she could

tell he was nervous as he scraped a hand through his hair. The stranger must have noticed, too.

"What's going on? Are you hiding something?" he asked.

Cain shook his head a little too quickly.

The stranger ignored Cain and surveyed his surroundings. "I sense a human nearby..."

His long, black coat with golden embroidery swayed as he strutted in her direction. She clasped a hand in front of her mouth to muffle even the slightest sound.

Cain got to his feet. "I've just fed and left the unconscious human lying over there. She might have woken up, but you need not worry about her." He spoke loud enough for her to hear.

The stranger turned to face him, cocking his head. "You don't look like you've fed."

"Her blood wasn't to my liking. I'll find another donor later."

"Whatever. I don't want you feeding in my territory." He huffed.

Cain went back on his knee, bowing his head. "Of course. I'm sorry, Lucious."

"Don't forget to keep me posted on your progress."

"I will."

Lucious vanished without another word.

Cain waited a few minutes before calling her out of her hiding place. "Are you okay?" he asked.

She nodded slowly. "Was he the one you told me about?"

"Yes. Lucious is a prince in our world, so I have to treat him accordingly. He's vicious, and it'd be bad if he found out about you. Although he himself isn't strong, he has powerful friends who have his back. The most prominent one is his father, our king."

"I got a terrible vibe off him. And I had no idea there's a vampire king—or prince. Is it more of a symbolic figure?"

"The king is the ruling power—at least here in Europe. I'll tell you more about it another time. For tonight, I've had enough of Paris."

"Me too. I need a shower."

He chuckled. "Let's return, then."

She went into his arms, and he teleported them back home. After a hot shower, she joined him in the comfy living room, snuggling against him while reading a book.

****

Something's off. Where am I? Pitch-black darkness engulfed her. Instead of lying on her soft bed, she lay on a cold, hard surface without a pillow. Lilah tried to sit up, but something restricted her movements. Chains fixed her hands, feet, and torso. An overwhelming sense of dread overcame her, and she felt like she couldn't breathe.

"Hello?"

Her voice echoed through the darkness. It sounded like she was in a small, closed off room. How had she gotten there? She'd gone to bed like any other morning since living with Cain.

"Is anyone there?"

Still no answer.

Where was Cain? He wouldn't put her in such a situation, as he'd promised to keep her safe. This didn't feel safe at all.

A terrifying string of questions ran through her head. Was he looking for her? Did he know she was missing? Would he come to her rescue? Did he even care? Would she die in this dungeon?

Countless hours passed while she lay in absolute darkness, frozen with fear. A dry throat and the growling of her stomach added to her desperation.

Footsteps approached, a door opened, and light fell into the room. The sparse illumination allowed her to discern the outlines of her surroundings. She was in a square room with no windows and only one door. A slim man stood in the doorway. *Oh shit.* Even though she merely saw his silhouette, she recognized him at once, as something about him gave her the creeps.

"Lucious," she whispered.

Chapter 9

A cold, arrogant laugh greeted Lilah. "I see my reputation precedes me. You have me at a disadvantage since I don't know who you are. What's your name?"

"Where am I?"

In less than a second, Lucious moved from the doorway to her side. Grabbing her chin, he pulled her face close to his. "I asked you a question, and you *will* answer me. And whenever you address me, you'll call me 'master.' Understood?"

His menacing tone sent chills down her spine.

"What the—" she started, but he punched her in the gut. She gasped. Her instinctual response was to clutch her stomach, but the chains kept her hands in place, cutting into her flesh.

"You're not to comment, and you're not to question me. Instead, you'll answer my questions," Lucious spelled out.

"Yes, *master*." She couldn't defy him. He was a vampire, and he'd chained her to a fucking table. She glared at him nonetheless.

"Better. So, your name?"

"Lilah."

"Well, Lilah…When I encountered Cain last night, I noticed he wasn't alone. Since he tried to hide your presence, you piqued my interest. I won't put up with him keeping secrets from me. To punish him, I'll make you my pet instead."

"*Pet*?" She curled her lips as she repeated the term, appalled.

He punched her again, and she writhed as searing pain spread through her body. "I didn't allow you to speak, did I? What did you think you were to a vampire? An equal? Humans are nothing to us. You're fooling yourself if you believe you were anything more than a pet to Cain. And don't even hope for him to save you. He'll never go against me for something so trivial."

She gulped. Was she nothing but a pet to Cain? She'd shared her life and her blood with him for months, and she believed he cared for her. Was it all a lie? Had he been playing games with her? Would he abandon her? He had mentioned he didn't want to be on Lucious' bad side. If he only considered her a pet, he wouldn't risk getting into trouble. He'd leave her with Lucious.

When her eyes widened in horror, a sardonic smile spread across Lucious' face.

"It's time for some fun." He ripped her nightgown off her body, leaving her trembling and almost naked. "Such nice, unblemished skin…So many spots to feed from."

Her burning cheeks didn't keep her from shivering. Without her nightgown, she was freezing.

Lucious leaned in close and inhaled her scent. She held her breath while he inspected her body. When he bit down on one of her bare breasts, she cried out, and a satisfied smile formed on his face. He didn't ease the pain of his bite. After her breast, he switched to her thigh, then to her wrist.

"Please stop," she whimpered.

"I'm just getting started." He laughed.

When he bit into her neck, a horrible burning spread through her body. Tears ran down her face when she realized her helplessness. Since Lucious didn't take too much blood, she could not even hope for unconsciousness as a release. Her only option was to resign and endure his torture.

After leaving throbbing wounds all over her body, he left her in complete darkness again. Would her life be constant suffering and torture until he ended it?

For hours, she lay on the cold stone table. Everything burned and ached while she fell in and out of consciousness. Her body desperately craved water. Considering her situation, dying of thirst wasn't her worst option, but forfeiting her life wasn't acceptable to her.

"Have you accepted your fate yet?" Lucious' icy voice brought her back to reality.

She nodded slowly. Her dry throat reminded her she was at his mercy. "Please, master…I've lost a lot of blood. Please give me something to drink, or I'll die."

"Will you, now?" he asked derisively. "Your blood doesn't taste too bad, so keeping you hydrated isn't an unreasonable request."

He fetched a bottle of water and emptied it over her mouth. Since she lay on her back, unable to lift her head, drinking wasn't an easy feat. She tried to gulp as much water as possible without coughing too much, but most of the cool liquid missed her mouth and wet her hair, face, and upper body.

With a smirk, he left her alone again. Wet, cold, and more miserable than before. Dying from thirst might have been the better option. She'd hoped for a different life when she'd stayed with Cain, but a human in a world of vampires was utterly helpless. Assuming otherwise had been stupid.

Plagued by desperate thoughts, she cried herself to sleep.

****

Two vampires, one tall and slim, the other one smaller with a bulky figure, woke Lilah when they entered the room. When she asked what they were doing, the tall one cut her off.

"Shut up, slave. No one allowed you to speak."

That silenced her. Did they consider her Lucious' slave? "Slave" sounded even worse than "pet."

After unchaining her, the bulky one threw her over his shoulder and carried her out of the room like a sack of potatoes. Exhaustion and pain kept her from focusing, so she barely noticed her surroundings as he transported her from what seemed like a basement dungeon to the higher levels of a medieval castle.

They arrived at an enormous hall with a big, golden throne and a smaller one next to it. Three stairs led up to the thrones, which allowed anyone sitting on them to survey the entire room. A long, red carpet led from there to a huge wooden door with golden ornaments on the opposite side.

There was also a door behind the big throne and another one close to the main entrance. Huge paintings, showing gruesome and bloody scenes, decorated the red velvet-lined walls. Marble statues depicting gargoyles and other mythical creatures stood on the marble floor.

About ten meters from the thrones, a huge cushion lay on the floor next to a wall. The vampire put her on the cushion and attached a collar around her neck. A short chain connected the collar to the wall. Since lying on a cushion was an upgrade compared to sleeping on the stone table, she didn't even protest. She curled up into a ball, hoping to warm her body.

Half an hour later, the door behind the thrones opened, and Lucious entered, followed by an old-looking vampire, whose posture demanded respect. He was taller than Lucious, with a strong build, a beard, and long, dark hair with gray streaks. While Lucious lounged on the smaller throne, he took a seat on the bigger one. They engaged in a heated discussion, which she couldn't grasp, as she barely held on to consciousness.

Lucious rose and made his way to her with two wineglasses in his hands. Squatting down in front of her, he grabbed one of her arms and bit into her wrist. She whimpered when her blood dripped into the glasses. Since he didn't bother to close the wound afterward, she clutched her wrist with her other hand to stop the bleeding.

Lucious returned to his throne and handed one glass to the older vampire, who looked at her for the first time.

"So you got yourself a new slave?" He sighed.

She didn't catch more of their conversation. Her mind drifted.

****

A loud crash, sounds of a struggle from outside, and the door broke with a deafening noise. Cain stormed into the hall, crossing the distance to the thrones within seconds. He paused five meters from them and bowed to the king before turning to Lucious.

Lilah's heart skipped a beat. Was she hallucinating or…Had Cain come to save her from hell?

Lucious feigned innocence. "What the hell are you doing here?"

"You know why I'm here. I want you to return what's mine," Cain snarled.

"I don't know what you're talking about."

After watching Cain's entrance with mild interest, the older vampire joined the conversation. "Cain, can you enlighten me what this is about?"

He took a deep breath, turned to the older vampire, and bowed his head. "I'm sorry for the disturbance, Your Majesty. Your son stole from me." Tilting his head in Lilah's direction, he said, "The human girl over there belongs to me. Lucious took her from me less than two days ago. I want her back."

Belongs to him. Cain's words made her stomach flutter with excitement.

"He's lying," Lucious interjected.

"So much ruckus about a human. Can either of you prove your claim on her?" the king asked.

"Let's ask her," Cain proposed, turning to face her. Compassion flickered across his face when their eyes met. "Tell us, Lilah, am I telling the truth? Did Lucious kidnap you from my home?"

While keeping her eyes locked with Cain's, she collected her strength to lift her head and nod. "Yes."

"Objection!" Lucious said. "Forcing a human to say whatever he wants is surely no challenge for Cain. His claim is ridiculous."

Cain shook his head. "You're pathetic. Why should I make up such a claim? If you don't return her, I'll take her back by force."

"As if—"

Cain cut him off. "As if I could beat you? You know I can. You're weak and not worthy of your title." His fists were shaking at his side.

The king sighed. Even Lilah could tell Lucious had nothing but a big mouth and a short temper.

Lucious leaped to his feet and drew a sword, which he'd stashed next to the throne. The ruby adorning the golden hilt of the weapon glinted as he raised it to storm at Cain, who defended himself with his own sword. Lucious furiously slashed at him, but he parried every attack with ease.

Without even trying, Cain pushed Lucious back until he had him with his back against a wall. "What will you do now? Will you call for help and prove my theory? You are nothing but a spoiled brat who can't fight on his own."

"Don't you dare!" Lucious' face contorted with anger. "You seem to forget who you're dealing with. I created you. You have no right to defy me."

Wait, what? Lilah blinked. If Lucious turned Cain into a vampire, how did they end up with such an estranged relationship?

"Strength gives me every right," Cain snapped. "In our world, only the strong survive. You taught me that."

"I gave you life. You should thank me on your knees for existing!"

Cain scoffed. "Thank you? Why? I never asked for this curse. You turning me is another good reason to kill you."

Out of nowhere, the king squatted in front of Lilah. She gasped and slid closer to the wall.

"It's okay," he whispered. "I don't aspire to hurt you. Will you help me de-escalate their conflict?"

The warm smile on his face tempted her to believe his words, so she nodded.

"Good girl. I'll take a sip of your blood to see the

truth in your memories, okay?"

Since she was in no position to refuse, she nodded again.

The king brought her hand to his mouth, pricked her fingertip on his fang, and licked the forming drop of blood up. While it dissolved on his tongue, he closed his eyes and furrowed his brows in concentration.

He swallowed and took another look at her, as if seeing her for the first time. "I'm sorry for my son. I promise you'll get out of here alive, but I have to use you to get their attention now."

"Any last words?" Cain's voice filled the hall as he pressed Lucious against the wall, his hand right above Lucious' heart.

The king rose to speak. "I wouldn't do that if I were you—" He destroyed the collar around Lilah's neck and lifted her up with one hand around her throat, leaving her feet dangling in the air. "—or your reason for coming here might not survive the next minute."

Cain froze.

The pressure on her throat made it hard for her to breathe, and she coughed for air.

Lucious chuckled.

"Shut up," the king bellowed before fixing his gaze on Cain. "Cain, I don't think you want to start a war here tonight, do you?"

"I don't want to, but I'll fight for what's mine. And I'll protect her with my life."

"I can see that. And yet, I hope we can solve this conflict peacefully," the king said. "I know you're telling the truth, and I appreciate your skills and the work you do for us. Thus, I'm willing to overlook your unseemly behavior in court today. If you release Lucious, I'll let you take her home, and we'll forget about the incident."

"What about him?" Cain asked.

"I'm sure he's learned his lesson. I apologize for the trouble he's caused, and I'll keep him out of your way."

Cain nodded and let go of Lucious, who sank to the floor. When the king put Lilah down, she slumped onto the cushion. Cain appeared by her side, shrugged off his coat, and draped it across her shoulders.

"Thank you. I'm glad we came to a peaceful solution," he said, taking in the damage Lucious had done. "Should he ever lay his hands on her again, nothing will stop me from taking his heart." He picked her up and held her in his arms as she snuggled against him.

"Fair enough," Lilah heard the king say before she drifted into a deep sleep. Cain's familiar scent gave her a sense of safety, and nothing kept her from giving in to her exhaustion.

Chapter 10

Her bed was warm and soft, and Lilah did not want to open her eyes. Once she did, she spotted Cain sitting next to her. A relieved smile spread across his face when her eyes met his.

"How long was I out?" she asked.

"You've slipped in and out of consciousness for three days."

"Three days?" Her voice shook, and she checked her body. Lucious' bite marks had vanished, and she wore fresh pajamas. "Well...I feel okay now."

"You should," Cain noted dryly. "I've given you quite a lot of my blood to heal you. Vampire blood can only heal physical wounds, though. Dealing with the emotional scars is a different matter."

"I'll be okay," she said weakly. Memories of pain and horror would torment her for a long time. Her mind wandered back to the throne hall, and she recalled Lucious' comment about giving life to Cain.

"So...Lucious turned you into a vampire?" she asked. "How did your relationship turn out...like this?"

An emotion flickered across Cain's face. She almost didn't catch the pain in his eyes as he looked away and took a deep breath.

"You wish to know my story? Fine. After what you've been through, you deserve to know more about my past with Lucious. Let's get you something to eat first and then chat in the living room. I'm sure you're starving."

Her stomach growled at the mention of food—she hadn't eaten in over five days. "Food sounds like an excellent idea."

He scooped her up in his arms.

"What are you doing?" she exclaimed. Despite her protest, her heart frolicked at his unexpected proximity.

"Making sure you don't overexert." He grinned as he carried her into the kitchen.

With a sandwich in hand, she curled up in a big blanket on the living room couch. He planted himself on the other end and told her his story.

"Shall I start with my childhood?"

She nodded while chewing her food.

"I was born in 1603 in a village in the Kingdom of Hungary. My mother died while giving birth to me, and I never knew my father. The church took pity on me. The local priest took me in and raised me like a son. He taught me to believe in God. I prayed to Him every day, and I lived a humble and righteous life in order to go to Heaven when I died."

"So you were religious?" she mumbled with a full mouth.

A sad smile formed on his lips. "I still am. I mean, I still believe in God, although He forsook me a long time ago. Lucious kidnapped me around the time of my thirteenth birthday. He was a newly turned vampire, and instead of fulfilling his duties as prince, he abused his power to torment humans for fun. I knew he was something dark, something different. My beliefs fascinated him, and he took pleasure in shattering them.

"My prayers and my precious rosary, which the

priest had bestowed on me for my birthday, didn't protect me from Lucious. I ended up in one of the darkest cells in his castle. God had abandoned me, but I kept praying. I prayed to God to let me see the light of day again. I prayed to God to punish him for his sins. Finally, I prayed to God to release me from my life. Yet He never answered my prayers. After years of suffering, I couldn't take it any longer and tried to end my life."

"Years?" She shuddered. "I couldn't have endured his torture for years."

"Taking my life was my last resort since it ensured I'd go to Hell. Eventually, I figured Hell could not be worse than Lucious' torture. But he found me in time to keep me from dying. That night, he turned me into a vampire so I would never escape his clutches."

His hands clenched into fists, and he took a deep breath.

"When I awoke, I wasn't in my cell. With no one nearby, I thought I could escape. I hadn't realized he'd turned me. I assumed Lucious had found me after my attempted suicide and thought me dead. As I didn't want to let this chance go to waste, I ran. The castle wasn't far from the church where I grew up. I fled there, seeking refuge, and ran into the priest who had raised me.

"Although six years had passed, he recognized me at once. He also saw something else in me, something evil. Instead of welcoming me, he called me a demon and begged me to stay away from him. It shattered me when the man who had been like a father to me tried to shove me away. I explained how I'd suffered all those years, and I told him I'd never strayed from God's path, but he didn't listen. Then I noticed the hunger in me." A shiver went through his body.

"You don't have to keep talking if the memory is too painful," she whispered.

He shook his head and continued, "A hunger unlike anything I'd ever felt overwhelmed me. When I came to my senses, I'd ripped the priest's throat open and fed on his blood. For my sins, God condemned me to roam the earth as a monster. I knew I'd never be welcome in Heaven again. Lucious found me then, and my desperation pleased him. I didn't know what to live or die for. Nothing mattered. He brought me back to his castle, where I served him. It took me years to get my focus back. Even though God had damned me, I wouldn't let it be the end of me. I vowed to make Lucious pay for what he'd done."

"How?"

"I trained hard, getting stronger every day for the mere goal of defeating him. He didn't even notice my progress. His father, however, did, and he was well aware of my intentions. When the king called me to him, he confronted me about my plans. Instead of chastising me for plotting against Lucious, he asked what I'd do after going through with my revenge and whether I was aware of the consequences.

"I knew nothing about the powerful forces standing behind Lucious. The king would be obliged to kill me for my betrayal, as would his other allies. I'd spend the rest of my cursed life running from certain death. As I'd already sinned beyond reason, dying wasn't an option. I couldn't face God's judgment after what I'd done."

"Why did you almost kill Lucious now and risk certain death?"

"Because I wouldn't have killed him for my sake. I'd have killed him for you, to save you from going through the same experiences. By killing him for me, I'd practically kill myself. And for what? Revenge? The satisfaction of paying him back for what he'd done? If I faced God after acting on those emotions, I'd deserve all the punishment He could give. If I kill and risk my life, I try to do it for the right reasons. Keeping you safe sounds like a good reason to me." He smiled at her.

"I feel flattered, but please don't throw your life away for me. I'm just a human."

"Your life is worth at least as much as mine. I'm not even alive."

"You look pretty alive to me." She smiled wryly. "What happened with you and the king? Did he punish you?"

"No. The king had developed a liking for me or maybe for my endurance and power. He offered me the possibility of choosing freedom instead of revenge, a life away from Lucious. In return for running errands for him, he kept Lucious off my back. With time, I learned to smother my wish for revenge and came to terms with what I am. My existence is a sin, and God won't even listen to my prayers. If I died, I'd be as far from Him as I could be. Thus, I keep living while suffering silently for every sin I commit."

She was speechless for a moment. His often playful demeanor hid his desperation well. Although his sadness sometimes shone through his eyes, he skillfully hid his true face. "Seeing the world through your eyes must be awful. At first, you suffered from what others put you through. Now, you blame yourself for what you have to do to survive. Stop blaming yourself for something you didn't choose. And don't be afraid of God's judgment if God never helped you."

"What an awfully simple way to view the world. You have neither seen what I've seen nor done what I've done. Otherwise you'd wish for God's forgiveness, too. It doesn't matter why. The point is, I've sinned. I'd already sinned before Lucious turned me. I lost my chance for salvation the moment I tried to kill myself. Since I don't dare to face my Creator to pay for my sins, I deserve to suffer every minute of my life. I don't expect you to understand that."

The finality in his voice didn't allow her to argue. She didn't understand his view on life. His power was astounding. Many people would give anything to become like him. Yet he considered his existence a curse, and her heart ached for him. Even though she could say nothing to convince him otherwise, she vowed to herself to change his dreary outlook on life.

Snuggling close to him, she whispered, "You've shown me life can be much more than what we take it for, so let me show you there's more to life than suffering."

His eyes widened as she placed a kiss on his cheek.

Chapter 11

"What was that about?" A cheerful, almost childish, inquiring look replaced his troubled expression.

Since he finally opened up to her, she would not condone any more walls between them. Although she'd kissed him on impulse, she'd been wishing to get closer to him for a while. Her horrible experiences with Lucious taught her how precious time with Cain was, and she yearned to make the most of it. Besides, she longed to feel something other than pain.

Did he feel the same way? She answered with a question. "What do you think?"

He pulled away. "I think you've suffered a trauma and don't know what you're doing."

She held on to his sleeve to stop him from moving too far away. "Maybe, but you're not doing so great yourself. You're putting on a mask most of the time, letting none of the hurt you're carrying inside show. What's wrong with comforting each other?"

"I need no comfort."

"You're not used to letting people into your life. How many people have you told your story before me? I'm convinced not even a handful know who you truly are. You're lonely, and you've been on your own for centuries. Even if you won't admit it to yourself, you've been searching for a companion to share your burden with. You took me in for that reason. So why don't we take whatever we have here to the next level?"

"It's true. I've taken you in because I've longed for a companion. Even though we've only shared a short amount of time, I treasure you. You're the only one who doesn't see me as a monster. I don't want to risk breaking our bond or take advantage of you when you're vulnerable." His voice thickened with emotion.

"I'm well aware of what I'm doing. I chose to stay with you, and I'm not going anywhere. If I kiss you, it's what I desire. The question is, what do *you* want?" She peered into his eyes and almost got lost in their depth.

He studied her intently. She meant every word. Ever since she'd first laid eyes on him, he'd captivated her. The more she saw of him—his cheeky side, his determination, his strength, and the burden he carried—the more he fascinated her. Something sprouted between them, although she wasn't ready to name it yet. Being with him made her whole and alive. And she longed to feel him in this moment.

"I haven't let anyone close to me in centuries," he said after a while, "but you're tempting me. Who am I to refuse you, my sweet, precious human?"

With a smile, he pushed her onto her back and captured her mouth with his. She closed her eyes to revel in the sensation. His passionate and demanding kiss stole her breath as his tongue invaded her mouth and danced with hers.

While he kept her preoccupied with their kiss, his hands traveled along her body, unbuttoning her pajama top. Her eyes opened with a gasp when he slid down to pay special attention to her breasts.

Sensations flooded her mind as he licked and sucked on both of her nipples, alternating between them. With his skilled tongue and his supernatural speed, they quickly hardened, and she panted.

"You're already breathless? I haven't even started," he teased.

"How about we even the playing field?" She tugged at his shirt.

With a grin, he obliged and stripped down to his shorts.

She marveled at his muscular body.

"May I bite you here?" He indicated her breasts.

"Yes, please." She didn't know what he'd planned, but she trusted him to override her awful memories with better ones.

With a playful smile, he bit down on her nipple. Pleasure spread from her breast to her entire body, and she cried out in ecstasy. While the first breast was still throbbing, he bit into the other one. The second wave of pleasure brought her over the edge, and her body spasmed.

"How about we take this into a bedroom?" he asked once her breathing had calmed down.

When she nodded, he picked her up and carried her up the stairs. He laid her on a huge, king-sized bed with black sheets, surrounded by red silk curtains straight out of a dark fairy tale. After one last inquiring look, he removed the rest of their clothes.

His fiery gaze explored her body with a different kind of hunger. When his eyes landed on her lips, she pulled him close. He claimed her mouth with his, and his hand slid down between her legs. After massaging her sweet spot, he entered her with two fingers, eliciting a moan.

She yearned to feel all of him, but he kept teasing

her. He trailed kisses down her body, paying close attention to each of her breasts before going farther down, until his mouth reached her core. She shivered in anticipation. He bent down and mercilessly licked and sucked on her nub, setting her entire body on fire, searing with sensation.

When he came back up, his mouth claimed hers as he entered her, filling her completely. He thrust into her again and again until first Lilah and then Cain found their release in an explosion of passion.

Thoroughly satisfied and content, she cuddled up to him. As long as he remained by her side, the horrors of the past nights didn't matter. The sky was getting light, though. She knew he'd retire soon, leaving her all alone for the day.

"Please don't let me sleep alone," she whispered. She needed to hold on to the feeling of security his presence gave her.

He searched her eyes for a moment.

"I won't." He placed a kiss on her forehead.

She almost protested when he got up, but he merely pulled a curtain in front of the windows before lying back down and covering both of them with a big blanket. Her heart swelled with happiness as she fell asleep in his arms.

****

Lilah woke to find Cain next to her. He leaned on his left arm and watched her thoughtfully.

"Morning." She smiled shyly. The memory of his touch was fresh on her mind. Where would they go from here?

"You know…I could have lost you at court." His lip trembled slightly as his eyes searched hers. "So if you wish to endure by my side, you must become stronger and more capable of defending yourself. Although I'd understand if you preferred to return to your old life."

She stared at him. Why would he even think she wanted to leave? "I'll never return to my old life. And you're not getting rid of me." She shot him a wicked grin. "I'd love to become stronger...But how can I, a human, ever defend myself against a vampire?"

"I've heard rumors about—" His brows furrowed while he tried to find a fitting word. "—experiments in the States. A group of vampires kidnapped human children and raised them while feeding them vampire blood and keeping them on a strict physical training schedule. The blood strengthens the children and quickens their progress.

"At the end of their teens, they are supposedly as strong as an average vampire. The concept of forcing a human child into such a life sounds horrific to me. However, the general idea of training combined with the effects of regular consumption of vampire blood might be the key to bringing a human to the level of a vampire. I don't know if it'll work or how much progress you can make, considering you're not a child anymore. But we could try...?"

"Being on par with a vampire...sounds awesome...almost too good. I've seen you fight and marveled at your power, so if there is even a little truth to these rumors—merely a chance it'll work—then I want to try it. It'll be a challenge, though. I've never done martial arts or excelled at physical exercises, but I've lacked motivation to try, until now. What will the training be like?"

"We must work on your speed, stamina, flexibility,

and strength. As a first step, we can combine running, lifting weights, and self-defense. With vampire blood added to your system, you should advance quickly and you won't suffer from muscle aches or exhaustion.

"Once we've brought you to a decent level, I can teach you a variety of fighting styles, from hand-to-hand combat like kung fu or karate to fighting with weapons like staves, swords, or throwing stars. If my blood heightens your senses, I can show you how to use them to your advantage. And once you've learned to hide your aura, you'll stand a chance against any vampire without special skills or too much fighting experience."

"Sounds like a long way to go," she murmured.

"The process might take years. It might not even work. It's an experiment, which will require your dedication for a long time. Are you up for that?"

"I'm willing to try, but I can't promise I'll see it through."

"Once you've started, I won't let you quit," he said with a devilish grin.

"Fair enough. I hate quitting anyway. When do we start?"

"Tomorrow. I'll grant you one more night of reprieve."

"Well, then, I know the perfect way to spend it." She pulled him close for a kiss.

Chapter 12

"Do you want juice with my blood?" Cain held a knife in one hand and a glass in the other.

Lilah almost choked on the last bite of her breakfast omelet. "You were serious about me drinking blood yesterday?" Wasn't there a less disgusting way for her to ingest it? "Can't I simply cut myself and let your blood enter my system through the wound or something?"

"Not if you aim to strengthen your body. The other way is only good for healing superficial wounds."

She grimaced. "Orange juice, please."

He put the glass on the kitchen table, filled it halfway with juice, and cut his palm with the knife. Several drops of blood dripped into the drink before his wound closed on its own.

"Drink," he said.

She took a whiff of the juice and cringed at its faint metallic smell. Since waiting wouldn't improve the taste, she downed the contents in one go.

"Do you feel anything?" he asked.

"Apart from the urge to retch? Not really."

"Okay. Let's find out how it affects your body during training. You better put on some weatherproof clothes…"

As a thin layer of snow coated the outside world, she dressed in a long coat and warm shoes. "How do we start?"

"Let's pretend I'm a big, bad vampire who craves your blood. You've escaped, so…now's your chance to run!"

She blinked. "Run? Where to? I don't want to get lost in the woods."

He chuckled and vanished from where he stood. In the next moment, arms grabbed her from behind and pulled her into a hug. "Wrong reaction," he whispered, sending a shiver through her body. "Your hesitation gave the big, bad vampire enough time to catch you."

"We haven't even started yet."

"Wrong again. You always have to be ready when facing a vampire." He released her. "Seriously, though, don't worry about getting lost. Getting away from me will be the real challenge."

He crossed his arms and watched her expectantly. After another glance at him, she ran.

Her legs felt lighter than usual, and even the cold air in her lungs didn't slow her down. She made her way through the trees, careful not to stumble or slip on the partially frozen ground. The occasional sounds of leaves rustling or twigs breaking kept her on edge, but she only had to worry about the vampire breathing down her neck.

After jogging for almost an hour, she had a stitch and paused. She'd run farther than she thought possible, but was it far enough for him to acknowledge her effort? As he expected her to get away from him, hiding seemed like a good idea. A nearby formation of large boulders offered shelter from searching eyes. She leaned against one of them and waited.

Cain turned up in front of her with a scowl on his face. "I told you to run, not to run and hide. Even without your footprints in the snow, hiding from a vampire is a foolish decision, unless you're capable of extinguishing your aura."

"Well, I needed a break."

"Do you think a vampire out for your blood will give you a break when you need one?"

"Probably not." She smiled sheepishly.

His expression softened. "Not too bad for a first try, though. The blood helped, eh?"

"I think so. But the effect is fading."

"You'll require much more blood to achieve any lasting improvements. Luckily, I've got another idea on how to feed it to you."

"How?"

He grinned and pressed her against the boulder as his mouth captured hers in a deep kiss. When she melted against him, he took a step back, leaving a liquid with metallic taste in her mouth.

"Swallow," he said.

She obeyed with a grimace.

"Better?"

"Not really, although this method is more fun. Where did you get the idea?"

"I often heal my bite marks by pricking my tongue on my fangs. It's less messy than cutting into my skin."

"Huh, clever." She touched the spot on her neck he usually fed from. "I've already wondered why you rarely leave a mark."

"Up for another run? I'll race you back home."

"You probably won't accept no for an answer, will you?"

"No, I won't." He grinned. "But I'll give you a head start."

With a sigh, she started running.

He was waiting inside when she arrived an hour later. "Ready for phase two of today's training?"

She eyed him warily. "I guess…"

"Follow me." He went to the basement door and opened it with a key.

She followed him down a stairwell into a fitness and training room filled with weight machines and various weapons. A giant tapestry depicting *The Last Supper* decorated the far wall. "Not what I expected down here," she muttered to herself. The mystery of where he usually slept remained.

Ignoring her comment, he explained how to use each of the machines, fed her a few more drops of blood, and left her training on her own until lunchtime.

After finishing her last exercise, she slumped onto the couch in the living room. Her muscles ached, and she didn't want to move another centimeter.

"Don't tell me I've already worn you out? The interesting part starts after lunch." Cain placed a paper bag with a mouthwatering smell in front of her. "I got you a potato casserole. Eat up."

She groaned inwardly but kept her mouth shut. Even if the training was a pain in the neck, he meant well. After all, they were training for her sake. She quickly finished her meal and met him in the basement for self-defense lessons.

Her training didn't get any less brutal in the following months. He woke her every evening as soon as the sun set. She got a few drops of his blood and ate breakfast before starting the night with a three-hour run through the forest, no matter the weather. Neither lightning, rain, snow, nor storm was an excuse for her to stay inside. After the run, she spent about two hours exercising with weights, followed by lunch and an intensive one-on-one combat training with Cain. He never went easy on her. Every time she didn't evade or block his attacks fast enough, she ended up on the floor. When she couldn't move, he gave her several drops of blood for her body to heal. When they finished around dawn, she had scarcely enough energy left to take a shower before falling asleep. Since he often kept her company in bed, she moved into the room with the king-sized "fairy-tale" one.

****

"The training isn't working," Lilah complained one night. "It's been four months, and I've made no perceivable progress."

On the other hand, surviving months of Cain's hellish training regime exceeded anything she'd thought her body capable of. The effect of his blood truly astounded her. And the kisses they shared when he fed it to her encouraged her not to give up.

He laughed. "You've made more progress than I thought possible in such a short amount of time. Let's go out. There's an assignment I've put off for too long. A group of hunters eradicated several young vampires, and now I have to take care of them. You can have a go at them, too, so we'll kill two birds with one stone."

"What? Kill them…?" she stammered.

"No, killing hunters is my burden to bear. Join me, observe their movements, and maybe spar with them. The difference in your abilities will astonish you."

She gulped. Could she fight against humans? Challenging hunters put her in less danger than fighting a rogue vampire, so it was the perfect way to test her progress. "Okay."

Cain offered her his hand and pulled her close once she took it. A few seconds later, they stood in a sparsely illuminated neighborhood. Yet he didn't let go of her hand.

"This place seems familiar. Where are we?" she asked.

"Hamburg."

"Oh, I've actually been here a few times with my parents. Who knew vampires lived in a city less than two hundred kilometers from where I grew up?"

"There are vampires in almost every big city, you know?" He chuckled. "We rarely stop for a chat with our donors, though."

After strolling through the streets of Hamburg for a while, she felt like someone was watching them. Distant footsteps revealed the location of their pursuers.

"Hunters?" she whispered.

"Very good." Cain smiled and squeezed her hand.

They walked a few more blocks and arrived at a closed off parking lot. Their pursuers followed, always staying one block behind.

Cain confronted them. "If you tried following us unnoticed, you failed."

"You think you can take us?" a black-haired hunter holding a gun shouted. "Think again!" He stormed into the parking lot with two other hunters—a bald man with a broadsword and a woman swinging a staff.

"Girl, get away from him. He's dangerous," the bald one said.

"I don't think so," she answered. "I know who he is. Unlike you, he doesn't attack people for no reason. So I'd rather fight on his side, thank you very much."

"People?" the woman asked, perplexed. "He's not a

person, he's a monster!"

Cain flinched slightly. Lilah clenched her fists as she positioned herself in front of him. She couldn't save those hunters from their narrow-mindedness. "If you want to kill him, you must get past me first."

"You're crazy," the man with the gun said. Yet he let his hands sink slightly, as if he were unwilling to shoot a human.

The woman readied her staff and charged at Lilah. "If I have to bring you down to save you, so be it!"

Lilah blinked a few times. Did the female hunter move slowly on purpose? She evaded the first three slashes of the hunter's weapon before going on the offensive. As the staff forced her to keep some distance, she tried to kick it away. Using the momentum from evading a hit, she attacked the woman with a roundhouse kick. She hit the woman's arm hard. The staff fell down with a *clank*, accompanied by the sound of breaking bones. The female hunter cried out in pain, sinking to the ground.

"What kind of monster are you?" The bald man charged at Lilah.

His broadsword intimidated her, but his movements were slower than hers. After evading a swing of the sword, she tackled him. They both fell, but she got to her feet faster than the hunter.

"All right, Cain," she said, "I've seen enough, and I get your point. They're yours now."

He nodded and went after the man with the gun, who beheld the scene with an open mouth. Grabbing him from behind, Cain bit into his neck, feeding on him until he dropped to the ground, dead.

Cain drew his sword and finished the other two

hunters off. To Lilah's surprise, she could discern each of his movements. Before she'd started her training, they were often nothing more than a blur.

"Why haven't I noticed this change before?" she asked.

"You've been working so hard, and I didn't want to spoil the surprise. Every day, I moved faster, hit harder, and kept you fighting longer. You simply didn't notice the rising difficulty. Even though you only consumed a few drops of blood every day, the power accumulated in your body."

"Are these improvements permanent?"

"Not necessarily. I believe the effects can last for months or even years, but they'll subside without a fresh supply of blood. They'll probably last longer if you hone your skills. Speaking of which, I think you're ready to start weapon training now."

"I'd love to. A staff looks fun..." she mused, inspecting the woman's weapon.

He shrugged. "Take it if you want to keep it as a memento."

She kept the staff, although she soon switched to using two silver-coated daggers in close combat and a silver-coated chain whip for long-distance attacks. These weapons proved more effective against vampires, and she could conceal them more easily.

Chapter 13

Apart from staves, daggers, and chain whips, Cain taught Lilah how to use swords, throwing weapons, and guns. They invested two weeks in each weapon before moving on to the next.

One night, she was working out in the basement when a loud knocking sounded from upstairs. Cain was out running errands, and he never knocked. Neighbors or salespeople didn't drop by either, as no road led up to his estate in the middle of nowhere. So who was at the door? Curiosity drew her to investigate.

She opened the door to find a young man with reddish-brown hair, a full beard, and rough facial features, wearing a long, beige coat, outside. There was something peculiar about him. Her skin tingled slightly in his presence, which led her to a simple conclusion.

"You're a vampire," she said.

He narrowed his eyes and lunged at her.

She sidestepped him without thinking, escaping his grasp by a hair. "What the hell! What have I done to you to deserve such a greeting?"

"Isn't it obvious?" He lunged at her again. "Since you're human, you shouldn't know I'm a vampire. You shouldn't even be here."

"Says who? You're the one who's trespassing." She ducked behind the couch to avoid his next attack.

"I'm trespassing? You're a hunter."

"Bullshit, I'm no hunter. I live here with Cain."

"And I'm supposed to believe you?" he scoffed. "You obviously don't know Cain. He's a friend of mine, and even though he might play with his food, he's not the type to get himself a pet. So cease your charade, hunter. I doubt you'd prevail over Cain, but I'll do him a favor and get rid of you."

Beads of sweat built on her forehead, and her pulse raced. It might still be another thirty minutes until Cain returned. Could she defend her life long enough? Since her only chance was to try, she pulled her curled up chain whip out of her pants pocket. Her opponent was unarmed, but his muscular build hinted at his fighting experience.

She struggled to keep her distance as they circled the couch. When he jumped over the piece of furniture, she slashed the whip at him. He evaded the first hit, but she kept attacking. After receding a few steps, he blocked the whip with one arm before charging at her. She retreated farther into the room until she bumped into something big.

The vampire threw himself at her with full force, but she ducked away. He crashed into the billiard table, shattering the wood. Yet he got up as if nothing happened. She tried to keep him away by spinning her chain whip, but he grabbed the other end of her weapon and ripped it from her hands. She gulped as a wide smile spread across his face.

It's not over yet. I'm not weaponless. Her hand clasped the handle of a dagger hidden in her belt while turning so he wouldn't notice it. When he tackled her, she rammed the blade into his stomach.

"Fuck you!" He growled while jumping back and

knocking over a lamp. Blood gushed out of the wound, spoiling the carpet.

His injury gave her a much-needed breather, and she took in the damage they'd done. *Cain won't be happy about this mess.*

As if her thoughts conjured him, Cain appeared in the living room. "What the hell is going on here?"

"You're back!" She let out a sigh of relief. "This guy knocked on the door, and when I opened it, he attacked."

"Explain yourself, Andrew." His eyes narrowed on the vampire.

Andrew frowned. "I assumed she was a hunter, so I wanted to get rid of her for you."

Cain chuckled. "And she almost got rid of you instead." His tone turned serious and threatening. "Don't make assumptions about my houseguests. Luckily, she was more than capable of defending herself. I wouldn't be having this conversation with you otherwise. Now get out of my sight before I finish what she's started."

Andrew clutched his bleeding stomach and looked bewilderedly from Cain to Lilah before he concentrated for a moment and vanished.

"Are you okay?" Cain asked.

She nodded. "I guess I had the element of surprise on my side...But I'm glad you showed up when you did."

"Speaking of surprises..." He rummaged through his coat pockets and pulled out an envelope. "I've got tickets for a late-night showing of that epic fantasy movie. You know, the one based on the book you devoured last month."

"Wait, they turned it into a movie?" She gaped at him with an open mouth before it turned into a wide smile. "Awesome!"

He looked at her with a tender expression. "I knew you'd be thrilled. The show starts in about an hour, which should give you enough time to get ready."

"Thank you!" She gave him a quick kiss before hurrying upstairs.

****

"So what's next?" Lilah asked at the beginning of their next training session. Her heart leaped at the prospect of learning how to handle yet another weapon.

"Learning how to fight with another weapon is a waste of time," Cain said.

"Why?" She pouted.

"You won't progress much more with our current training regime. You're fast, you're strong, and you've mastered a variety of fighting skills and weapons. Yet you still don't stand a chance against a skilled vampire."

"I'm not doing too bad against you anymore."

He laughed. "You know I'm still holding back. You're good—better than any other human, but vampires aren't human. People call us beasts and monsters because of our violent nature and our consumption of blood. I believe there's also a different reason. Unlike vampires, humans have abandoned their instincts. They react based on what they see, feel, or hear.

"If you wait for one of your five senses to register an enemy's attack, it might be too late. You have heightened senses thanks to my blood, but you rely on them too much. They're not perfect, and there's always the risk of losing one of your senses in battle. Being helpless because someone blinded you might prove deadly."

"Well, then…How do I strengthen my instincts?

How did it work for you when you became a vampire?"

"It's not something I've done, it's what I am. Becoming a vampire awakened my instincts. Instincts dominate all animals…no, all beings except for humans. It's about reacting to what's happening around you without thinking about it. I'm sure this ability slumbers in every human. The question is how to awaken it in you. You've learned to fight with heightened senses. Now, you'll learn how to fight without them."

"Without my senses? Should I put soundproof headphones and a blindfold on?" she joked.

"Good idea. Let's try it." He *wasn't* joking.

"I don't think—"

Before she could finish her protest, he vanished. He returned two minutes later with soundproof headphones and cloth, which they could use as a blindfold.

With a sigh, she covered her eyes with the cloth and put the headphones on. The silence was deafening and the darkness unnerving. How was she supposed to fight? After taking a deep breath, she concentrated on her surroundings. The air to her right prickled. Was this Cain's aura? "All right, come at me."

She doubled over with pain when he hit her in the guts. The origin of the tingling sensation had moved, but the realization came too late.

"Again," she said.

Even though she emptied her mind of all distracting thoughts, the result didn't change. The next few attempts were no different. After getting punched for the twentieth time, she was ready to quit. She took off the headphones and removed the blindfold with a groan. "It's not working. I don't know how to awaken my instincts."

"We're not done yet." He pulled her close and caught her mouth in a kiss, feeding her some blood.

After months of this routine, she didn't mind the taste any longer, and the wave of energy surging through her body felt fantastic. "Thanks," she mumbled. "Still, I'm not sure how to proceed."

"Try to find something primal and animalistic within you. A new sense telling you what's happening before it happens."

A new sense? Something animalistic? The image of a straying cat came to her mind. She put the blindfold and headphones back on and went down on all fours. Getting into the mindset of an animal might help her react like one. What would a cat feel? What did it think about? A cat focused on whatever caught its attention, whether it was a mouse, another cat, or a human. Or maybe a butterfly fluttering by. A cat noticed every detail. It didn't reflect on how to react to a stimulus. A cat simply reacted.

With her change of perspective, she perceived her surroundings differently. Somehow, she knew what was happening around her.

"I'm ready," she said.

When he went for a hit, she ducked, still too late, but unlike the last twenty times, the hit only grazed her.

After a few more days of training without sight or hearing, she got the hang of it. With the mindset of a cat, she crouched down on the floor and envisioned her surroundings before her inner eye while waiting for Cain to attack. Once he did, she dodged in time and even landed a hit on him afterward.

Her next challenge was using her instincts combined with her normal senses while utilizing everything she'd learned in the previous months to develop her own fighting style.

At the end of her training, her movements and demeanor were more akin to that of an animal than a human. Along the way, she learned to detect nearby vampires and gauge their strength.

To refine her skills and gain practical experience, she even accompanied Cain when he hunted renegade vampires.

Chapter 14

On a warm night at the end of July, Cain was lounging with a newspaper in the living room when Lilah returned from a brief run through the forest.

"Anything interesting happening?" she asked.

He looked up. "Just the normal human craziness. It's always good to stay up-to-date with current events."

"I guess...I've never cared for politics, finances, or whatever happened in an unknown part of the world." She'd inherited her disinterest from her mother, who never even watched the news. Unlike her mother, she also didn't care for celebrity gossip.

"You should," he reprimanded her. "Vampires aren't interested in which moron is running for president since we have our own ruler. But knowing about conflicts can be useful to stay far away from them. Finances are important for a good life, and an incident in a faraway country can sometimes be a clue to an assignment. I once hunted a renegade vampire for weeks, only to find the missing clue to his whereabouts in the paper. He'd left a bloody trail of bodies for humans to find."

She only listened with one ear. Her senses focused on a faint, supernatural aura somewhere in the surrounding forest. "Are you expecting someone?"

He shook his head. "Might be a messenger, though. I've heard nothing from court for a while."

"Since when do you get messengers from court? I've never seen one around here."

"You've never noticed them until now," he corrected her. "Messengers drop by once every few months. They're usually faster and less clumsy in their approach, though. Do you want to greet our uninvited guest?"

"With pleasure." She grinned. Chasing down the unknown vampire would be fun. Since she had her weapons on her, she headed straight for the door.

The vampire wasn't at the house yet, but she felt his leisurely approach. Calming her mind to hide her own aura, a skill Cain had taught her recently, she ran toward the unknown vampire. After two minutes, she saw him in the distance. The skinny, blond man strolled through the forest without paying attention to his surroundings. Hiding behind a tree, she waited for him to get close and then tackled him from the side. Since she slammed into the surprised vampire with full force, they both fell. While the vampire stared at her, frozen in shock, she rolled over, straddled him, and pressed her silver-coated dagger to a spot right over his heart. "What are you doing here?"

"I-I have a mess—a message to—to de-deliver to C-Cain," he stuttered.

Cain's laugh echoed through the forest. "Well-done. Better let him go now, or he'll pee himself."

She got up, walked over to Cain, and left the perplexed vampire lying more or less unharmed on the ground.

"Now," Cain addressed him, "you have a message for me?"

The vampire got to his feet and bowed.

"Yes, sir." His voice was shaking as he pulled a letter out of an inner pocket of his jacket. Going down on one knee, he offered it to Cain, who accepted it.

"Thank you. You can go now," Cain dismissed him.

The vampire got up, took another bow, and left on foot.

"Can't he teleport?" she asked.

"He's young. He hasn't mastered teleportation yet," Cain mused. "I wonder why the court appointed a vampire without teleportation skills as a messenger. Walking makes delivery unnecessarily time-consuming. It's fun to watch, but still…" His voice trailed off while he read the letter.

"What is it about?" She edged closer.

"An invitation to court," he said, frowning.

"What's wrong?"

"Nothing is wrong. It's a little…unexpected."

"Why? Haven't you been to court many times before?"

"*I* have," he said. "But they are not only requesting my presence. Word got out that you've joined me on my recent assignments. So, this invitation includes you. I don't know what to make of it. I've never heard of the king inviting a human to court."

"Huh." She leaned closer to get a better look at the artfully handwritten letters in red ink on parchment paper. "Is that a bad thing?"

"I'm not sure…Lucious might be there. Even if he isn't, the court is dangerous, especially for a human."

"Well, you taught me to protect myself," she argued. "Besides, Lucious doesn't scare me anymore. When push comes to shove, I'll stab him with my dagger."

He pursed his lips. "That's a bad idea…But since the

king requested your presence, I won't stop you if you wish to come along. Besides, a visit to court might be more fun with you around."

"Great!" She beamed at him.

"If you insist on joining, you need to learn basic vampire etiquette. I don't care for it, but there are certain formalities everyone should abide by."

"Vampire etiquette? Are you talking about stuff like bowing to another vampire?"

He nodded. "At court, such formalities are obligatory. Many vampires live by them all the time. You saw the messenger handing me the invitation, for example. Unless you're out for a fight, interactions with unknown vampires are formal. Powerful vampires expect weaker ones to treat them with respect, and weaker vampires have to obey. Otherwise, they risk getting killed or at least punished for their insubordination.

"A strict hierarchy defines our world, ruled by strength and blood. The king is at the top, followed by everyone he has sired and then their fledglings. Next are powerful vampires who've fought for their rightful place. The weaker a vampire, the more he or she has to bow to another. Humans are at the bottom of our hierarchy, although you might be an exception."

"Where are you in the hierarchy?" she asked.

"Further up than I'd care to admit," he hedged.

"Meaning what?"

After a moment of hesitation, he answered, "Lucious sired me a handful of years after the king turned him. Some rumors claim he transferred too much of the king's power to me by turning me so soon after his own transformation without mastering his power first. I don't know if there's any truth to it. Since Lucious is disproportionately weak, it doesn't sound too preposterous. Thus, some people say I'm related to the king by blood, and I don't have to bow to anyone except for the king and my sire."

"Wow, I didn't know I was living with royalty," she said cheekily, taking a mocking bow.

The next moment, Cain pressed her against a tree. "If I was anyone who cared for these formalities, I'd have your head for your impertinence."

"Show-off." She smiled at him. Her body tingled with desire at his display of superiority, and she used his proximity to press a kiss to his lips. "Don't worry, I get your point. I promise I'll behave around other vampires. I won't behave when I'm alone with you, though."

Before he responded, she leaned in to kiss him again. He opened his mouth to welcome her probing tongue. When she broke free to catch her breath, he let his mouth travel down to her throat.

"What am I going to do with you?" He chuckled before sinking his fangs into her skin. The heat from his bite spread like a raging fever through her body, inciting an uncontrollable blaze of arousal.

When he released her, she clawed at his clothes. "I crave all of you."

"Do you, now?" His hands wandered along her body, massaging her breasts through her clothes.

She combed her fingers through his hair to pull him close for another kiss. His hands found their way to her shorts, and he slowly pushed them down. Cool air brushed against her sensitive skin once her panties followed. Burning fire replaced the chill as he caressed her most sensitive spot with his thumb. Her moans and the slick, wet sounds of his fingers pushing into her echoed through the woods.

"More," she pleaded.

He withdrew his fingers to relieve himself of his pants. She gripped onto his shoulder for support as he pushed her up against the tree and impaled her with his heat. Pleasure seared through her as they became one in the heart of the woods.

Chapter 15

Two days later, Cain took Lilah with him to court. He didn't teleport directly into the throne hall, though. They appeared on a deserted road leading up a mountain to the castle, a magnificent building with turrets and battlements surrounded by four towers and a high wall.

"Come on," he said, "it's a short hike to the top."

She furrowed her brows as she followed him. "Why didn't we teleport into the castle?"

"Because it's not possible. A magic shield protects the castle and keeps almost everyone from teleporting. Only the king can teleport to and from the castle itself," he explained. "Besides, a walk is perfect to go over the etiquette again. Do you remember what I told you?"

She sighed. "Stop worrying." They'd gone over everything a hundred times.

"Please humor me."

"All right. In a nutshell, I'll mimic whatever you do. When facing the king, I'll kneel like you. I won't speak unless prompted, and I'll stay behind you at all times."

"Very good."

They walked the rest of the way in silence.

A vampire guarded the castle gate. He leered at her with hungry eyes before turning to Cain with a small bow of his head. "Welcome, sir. Do you have an appointment?"

Cain nodded. "Yes, the king is expecting us."

" 'Us'?" the guard repeated. "You can't mean to take your human pet with you, can you? For her safety, I'd advise you to leave her here."

Pet? She gritted her teeth. She'd love nothing more than to make him choke on his own words.

Cain chuckled. "You think she'd be safer with you? Truth be told, I'd be more worried about your safety than hers if you tried anything. However, the king has requested her presence. So if you'd be so kind as to lead us to him?"

The guard gaped at them with an open mouth. Without another word, he bowed and led both of them inside.

They traversed beautiful halls decorated with golden statues and priceless but disturbing paintings of massacres and demonic creatures. The combination of antiques and artwork gave the impression of exploring a museum. They passed several guards on their way. Most of them eyed her with curiosity.

"Please wait a moment," the guard said when they arrived at a gigantic door.

He slipped inside to announce their arrival. When he returned, he opened the door for them and bowed deeply. "You may see the king now."

She recognized the enormous hall with the two thrones at the end. Except for the king sitting on the big throne, no one else was present. There was no sign of Lucious. She let out a breath she hadn't realized she'd been holding.

Cain approached the throne and kneeled with his head bowed. She followed his example, always staying a meter behind him.

"We're here as summoned, Your Majesty," he said.

"Thank you for coming." The king smiled warmly. "And I'm glad you brought your pet along. I'd hoped to meet again under better circumstances."

Again with the "pet." Cain never used the term, and she didn't think he considered her one. But every other vampire they'd dealt with had. Why? Since an audience with the king wasn't the best time to broach the subject, she swallowed her anger.

"Her first visit to court was less than ideal. I'm still sorry for the fuss I caused," Cain said.

The king shook his head. "I can see she's important to you, and I'm glad you've found something to care for. It saddens me that I haven't seen you in court lately, though. From what I've heard, you've spent quite some time training her, so I wanted to witness the results. Apparently, she's become an asset."

"I've merely taught her to defend herself."

"Being able to bring down vampires is more than defending oneself." The king chuckled and turned his gaze on her. "What's your name?"

She hesitated for a moment. Was it okay for her to answer? Since Cain said nothing, she did. "Lilah, Your Majesty."

"Lilah," the king said, "come closer, please."

As his request broke the protocol Cain had taught her, she didn't know what to do.

"It's okay, go ahead," Cain said.

She got to her feet, took a few steps, and kneeled next to him.

"Come closer," the king repeated.

Lilah glanced at Cain, who nodded in encouragement. She got up, passed Cain, and stopped right in front of the three stairs leading up to the thrones.

"Closer," the king said.

Tentatively, she took the three steps up to the throne and kneeled at his feet, eyeing him expectantly.

The king leaned over to her and lifted her arm up to his face, smelling her skin.

"May I?" he asked, addressing Cain.

She saw Cain shrug out of the corner of her eye.

"It's her choice," he said.

The king gazed at her. "Well?"

Well, what? She blinked a few times and searched his face for a clue. Realization hit her when her eyes fell on his fangs. "Go ahead."

The king lowered his head to bite into her wrist. He took three sips of her blood while numbing the pain. After closing his eyes for a moment, he pricked his tongue on one of his fangs and licked the wound to heal it. She watched him the entire time.

"It's unnerving when your food's looking at you while you're eating." The king grinned. "Thank you. You can return to Cain now."

She blushed before she could stop it. After taking another bow, she returned to Cain, kneeling down at his right side. She'd passed the distance in less than two seconds, showing off her superhuman speed.

"She's quite something," the king said to him. "I can taste the power you've fed her. I didn't expect our blood to have such an effect on humans."

"She's trained hard. Her progress is largely due to her determination."

"I'm glad she thrives in our world. She'll make an impressive and fun vampire one day," the king suggested.

Her heart beat faster at the king's words. She loved

the idea of becoming a vampire, living forever at Cain's side.

Cain crushed her hope. "Maybe, but I have no intention of turning her. I swore a long time ago to never create a vampire. Since I enjoy her human company, there is no reason for me to change my conviction."

She tried to hide her disappointment, but the king gave her a knowing smile.

"We'll see." He chuckled, and Cain stiffened next to her. "I also have a new assignment for you."

"What is it?" Cain asked.

"We've got reports of vampires disappearing from the center of Rome. No one knows why. Maybe they're up to something shady, or hunters killed them. Whatever the reason, I want you to investigate and obliterate any potential problems."

"As you wish." Cain bowed his head, and the king dismissed them.

Chapter 16

After leaving the castle, Cain teleported straight to Rome with Lilah to get a first impression of the situation. Even in the middle of the night, the air was humid, and breathing felt hard. Illuminated ruins and buildings offered an enchanting sight, but she paid them no mind as they explored the city.

"You're awfully quiet," he noted after a while.

She shrugged. Cain's words still occupied her mind. Why wouldn't he even consider turning her?

"What's wrong?" he asked.

"I'd love to become a vampire one day."

He sighed. "Why do you long for death?"

"I don't long for death. I long for eternal life." *With you.*

"Eternal life? It's a damned life. Forced to walk this earth forever while living on the lives of humans and watching everyone and everything around you wither. Is that what you wish for?" His question sounded like an accusation.

"With you by my side, I won't have to watch *everyone* wither. And it's not a damned life. See your life for what it is. You're fast, you're strong, and you can do things humans only dream of. You'll never die, and you won't get sick." She nibbled on her lower lip. "Things are changing, but you'll experience more than any human could hope for. Why don't you want to share your amazing life with me?"

He slowly shook his head. "It's not about not wanting to share my life with you. My life is a curse. It seems amazing to you because you only see what you wish to see. You don't see the countless lives I've taken, regardless of whether I extinguished them for an assignment or because I couldn't control my thirst for blood." His voice broke, and his chin quivered. "You don't know what it feels like when everything around you changes and everyone you've known has died. When you've lived as many lives as I have, life is an endless journey of despair and loneliness, where nothing matters anymore."

She tensed and breathed out noisily. "Nothing matters? So...I don't matter? Sharing your life with me for over a year doesn't matter? Watching me grow old and die one day won't matter?" Her voice raised in volume with every word.

"In the grand picture, it won't. It's the way of life, and I've learned to accept it," he answered in a toneless voice.

"So, you'd rather watch me die than give me the opportunity to live forever...because it's the way of life?" she screamed at him, but he avoided her gaze. "Look at me when I'm talking to you!"

His shoulders slumped as he faced her, and his voice drowned in emotion. "I don't want to watch you die. But the thought of damning another soul to wander this gruesome world forever is unbearable to me."

"It's *my* soul," she argued. "As long as I'm fine with walking this world forever and living a damned life, you should be fine with it, too."

"But I'm not." He raised his voice. "And I'll never

be. I'll never turn a human, no matter who, no matter the consequences. Don't ask me again."

"Or what?" she challenged him. When he stared at the ground, she persisted. "The more I experience of your world, the more I long to become like you, see the world like you, and walk next to you until the end of time. I know what you've gone through, and I know vampirism feels like a curse to you, but it's not. If you hadn't become a vampire, I wouldn't have met you. You'd have died long before my birth. So, I'm glad you are what you are. Please give me a chance to prove to you it's not a curse."

In the next moment, he held her by the throat, lifting her up into the air with one arm. "You don't understand what you're talking about. Stop asking for death, or I might give it to you. Permanently." His eyes seemed feverish, like an unruly sea of pain and desperation.

She couldn't breathe. She struggled and kicked at him to break free, but to no avail. After several long seconds, he threw her to the ground.

As soon as she stopped coughing and gasping for air, she shouted at him, "What the hell do you think you're doing?"

"Showing you what you asked for: death. Becoming a vampire is dying. Don't ask for things you don't want."

"If death is the price I must pay, I'll pay it." She wouldn't give in. They were talking about *her* life.

"I can see we're not getting anywhere," he said, running his hand through his hair. "And I want you to understand what's at stake, so I'll make you an offer. Fight me with everything you've got. If you win, I'll grant you your wish and turn you into a vampire. If you lose, I'll take your life." He closed his eyes for a second as a shudder went through his body. "But if you're not ready to put your life on the line, I never want to hear another word of it."

"Fight you in a life-or-death match? I don't want to throw my life away! I know I don't stand a chance against you. You're not giving me a fair choice here."

"No, I'm not, but it's good to see you're not completely suicidal." He exhaled loudly. "This situation is my fault for bringing you into this world and putting your soul at risk. A human can't handle the taste of a vampire's power without becoming obsessed with it."

"You're becoming a bit melodramatic here."

Without a warning, Cain pulled her close and teleported them to another location.

"What? Where are we?" she asked, still caught in his sudden embrace.

"Where we started," he whispered before letting her go.

"Huh?" She glanced around. They were in her hometown, on the street where she'd met Cain for the first time. Or rather she was, because he had vanished.

"What the fuck? Are you kidding me?" she shouted into the night.

No answer.

"Cain?"

Still no answer.

She usually felt Cain's presence. He wasn't nearby any longer.

"You can't leave me here! Come on, it's not funny!" Desperation painted her voice. He wouldn't send her back to her old life, would he?

She kept screaming his name for minutes.

Minutes turned to hours.

Finally, she sank to the ground, sobbing.
He'd abandoned her.

Part II

JOURNEY

Break away, tempted
by the waxing moon's promise.
Always. Forever.

Chapter 17

Lilah found herself at her mother's doorstep. Tulips and boxtree bushes shaped like balls, pyramids, and cones decorated the front yard of the small, semidetached house. Everything felt familiar but also very wrong. Should she ring the bell? How would her mother react?

She hadn't expected to return, so how should she explain her absence? Did she have anywhere else to go? After pacing in front of the door for half an hour, she rang the doorbell and waited, but nothing happened. Why didn't anyone answer the door?

With a loud beeping, a garbage truck pulled up in front of the house and collected the wastepaper. Was it still early morning? Since her mum often slept in, she must have missed the sound of the bell. She rang one more time.

After several minutes, her mum opened the door with a yawn. She froze and gaped at her for a moment. "Lilah? How? Where have you been? Oh God...I...I thought..." Sobbing, she threw her arms around her daughter.

A wave of guilt hit her, and tears welled up in her eyes. "I-I'm sorry."

"I'm so glad you're safe. Please, come in. I'll make you a hot cup of tea." Without waiting for an answer, her mother ushered her inside and into the living room.

She settled down on the couch. Even though nothing had changed, this house didn't feel like home.

Her mum returned with two cups of chamomile tea. "For our nerves...I'm sure we both need it."

"Thanks."

"You look good...really healthy."

She remained silent as she studied her mother's appearance. Her mum had lost weight, but not in a good way. Her usually well-styled hair was a mess, and the pajamas she wore had seen better days.

"I know I haven't taken good care of myself," her mother confessed. "I've missed you, and I've searched for you for so long. What happened? You didn't come home, turned off your phone, and left no trace of where you went. Was it my fault? Did I drive you away? Or did someone kidnap you?"

"Shush." She tried to calm her. Her mum always talked too much when nervous or emotional. "It wasn't your fault...It wasn't anyone's fault. I was looking for my place in this world and found so much more. A place to call home, someone to share my life with, and...love."

Love? She couldn't deny the feeling, although she'd never admitted it out loud before. Her heart felt like breaking, but this wasn't the time to fall apart. "It felt right, so I left everything and everyone I knew behind without looking back. I'm sorry for worrying you, though."

"I'm happy you found your place, but why did you vanish off the face of the earth?"

"Didn't you get my goodbye letter?" *Had Cain truly delivered it?*

"I did, but...A letter? I'm your mother, for God's sake! For all I know, someone forced you to write it. And it revealed nothing about what you were doing! Why cut me out of your life?" A note of hysteria crept into her voice.

"Mum..." Lilah averted her gaze. "I'm sorry. There are things I can't explain. You wouldn't understand."

"Try me!"

She shook her head. "I can't...Cutting all ties to my former life paved the way for the life I desired. I didn't mean to vanish, but...in retrospect, it was what I needed."

"You needed to run away from me?"

"Mum, no..." She sighed. "My decision wasn't about you. I'm sorry if I hurt you...I wasn't happy with my life and the choices I had. Leaving all behind felt good."

Her mother sipped her tea. "So, what kind of life did you lead? What have you been doing?"

How could she answer the question without sounding like a madwoman? According to most people, vampires didn't exist. Besides, their lives depended on secrecy, and she would not betray Cain's trust. "I met a guy..." She stared at her cup. "He's...special, and he took me to a whole different world. I—"

Her mum interrupted her. "What are you saying? A different world? Who is he? I've always told you to find a guy, but I meant a normal one. Someone who takes care of you."

"I know *you* long for a normal life with a nice guy by your side, Mum. But I don't. I'm different, and I don't like normal. It's boring."

"What have I done wrong?" Her mother ran her hands through her hair. "Why did you turn out like this?"

"Nothing, Mum." She clasped her mother's hand. "I

had a wonderful childhood, and thanks to you, I've grown up to be independent. I don't want to live like everybody else."

Her mum withdrew her hand. "Why have you returned to me now if you're so happy in your other life?"

"Well…" How could she explain without revealing too much? "Our plans for the future didn't match…When I asked him to let me stay by his side for eternity, he abandoned me." She grimaced. *Ugh. Sounds like a declined marriage proposal.*

"I'm sorry, honey." Her mother's features softened. "But it's for the best…I don't think he was good for you."

"No…You don't understand…I…It's all my fault." She swallowed. "I can't give up on him. I don't know how, but I'll change his mind…even if I have to fight him for it."

"What are you talking about? No man treating you like that is worth fighting for. You'll find another one."

"I won't ever find someone like him."

"Someone better than him."

She shook her head. There was no use arguing about it, though. She needed time to figure out how to proceed. "Is it okay if I stay for a while?"

"Of course, honey." Her mum hugged her. "You can stay as long as you want—this *is* your home! I'm so glad you're back."

"Thanks, Mum. Is my room still…?"

"Everything is as you left it."

"Perfect. I need to lie down for a while…"

"Sleep well, honey." Her mother kissed her on the cheek.

As she climbed the stairs, her legs became heavier with every step. Was she really back in her old life—the life she never wanted? How could she go on without him? And why did the people she cared about the most always leave her? It was her fault this time, wasn't it? Once she arrived in her room, she collapsed into bed and let her tears flow.

Chapter 18

Emptiness. Pain. Days blended into each other as Lilah stared at the ceiling of her room. She lacked the energy to get out of bed. What for? She'd lost her one chance at happiness.

The door opened, and her mother entered with a bowl in her hands. "I made chicken soup." She put it on the bedside table.

Lilah didn't even glance at her. "Thanks."

"I'm glad to know you're right here, but…you've barely moved in days! This isn't healthy, honey. I worry about you."

"I know…" She sat up and stared at her mother without really seeing her.

"You need to go out into the world. Why don't you look for a job to get routine into your life?"

"I'll think about it."

"All right." Her mum smiled. "I'm off to work now. Let me know if there's anything I can help you with."

"I will. Thanks, Mum."

If she earned some money, she could travel to Rome and look for Cain. But what would she say if she found him? Could she convince him to take her back? Did she want to return after their argument? Could she deal with growing old next to him while he stayed forever young? Too many questions, but finding a job was a good start. She trudged from her bed to her desk and turned on the

PC.

Several messages popped up. Julia had reached out to her many times during the past months. Amanda had also sent her a couple of reports on her journey through Australia with a collection of stunning pictures. She didn't feel like answering either of them.

Instead, she scanned the internet for job ads in her region while spooning her soup. Even though she'd finished school, finding a well-paying job with no vocational training wasn't easy. Since she preferred working nights, she applied at a security firm looking for guards on short notice.

****

A smile played on Lilah's lips as she strutted home after her job interview three days later. The astounded expression on her new boss's face still amused her. He'd asked for a demonstration of her skills, but he hadn't expected her to disarm and subdue the other guard in a matter of seconds. Like most vampires, humans tended to underestimate her.

What if Cain underestimated her, too? The thought made her pause, and she clutched her chest. What if she could best him in a fight one day? He intended to deter her with his offer, but…what *if* she won against him and forced him to turn her? Even if he resented her at first, she'd have eternity to show him how much better spending forever together could be.

She didn't stand a chance against Cain yet, but what if she enhanced her skills even more? She'd already beaten the odds once when she became as strong as a mediocre vampire thanks to Cain's training. Without vampire blood to boost her power, or a decent sparring partner, her chances were slim.

Then again, according to Cain, vampires lived in almost every major city, so there had to be someone out there to help her obtain the power she lacked.

With her new goal in mind, the future didn't look as grim.

****

After three months of saving every penny she had earned, Lilah quit her job. She could not endure another uneventful shift at work while the world passed her by. Even if her path didn't lead her back to Cain's side, she had to set off to find her destiny. She packed a backpack with her chain whip, comfy fighting clothes, a blanket, toiletries, food, and the money she'd earned in cash, strapped her daggers to her body, and put on a long coat.

Except for her passport, which she required for crossing borders to different countries, she left identifying or trackable items like credit cards or the brand-new phone she'd bought for work behind. Saying goodbye to her mother was her final challenge.

"Hi, Mum." She waited in the doorway to the living room.

Her mum unglued her eyes from the enormous flat-screen TV to smile at her. "Hi, honey. Everything all right?"

"I'm leaving." Unlike her stomach, her voice didn't quiver.

"Leaving?" Her mother muted the TV. "Where are you going?"

"I don't know yet, but I know I won't return. I don't fit into this life."

"What are you saying? You've found a well-paying job, even though I still think it's not suited for a girl, and you can stay here and save up money until you rent your own place. Why isn't the life you're living enough? There are many handsome boys around. Why don't you give any of them a chance? You can start a family and be happy."

"Oh Mum, I'm sorry." She sagged onto the couch next to her mother. "The life you picture is not the life for me. I yearn for so much more. To come closer to my dreams, I need to leave everything behind. So…this is goodbye…for good."

"For good?" Her mum choked on the words. "What do you mean?"

"Once I'm gone, I won't return."

"But why does it have to be for good? I don't want to lose you. Not again. Let me come with you!" A tear ran down her cheek.

Lilah shook her head as she lowered her eyes. "You can't. It's too dangerous for you, and taking you along puts me in danger. You're made for the life you're living. A normal life. And you've raised me well enough to find my own path. So please, let me."

"Why does your path lead you away from here?"

"It just does. You want me to find happiness, don't you?" She swallowed hard.

"I do. But why can't you find happiness here, with me? Will you at least call me once a week to let me know you're okay?"

"No…I won't take my phone along."

"Why?"

"Because I might endanger everyone around me by broadcasting my location. Besides, if someone dangerous got a hold of my phone, they could find you through it."

"What kind of life makes you worry about such

things? Why do you long to live in such a world?"

"Mum, please. I've made my decision." She pressed her lips together.

"Even if you can't use your phone, why don't you call me from a pay phone now and then?"

The request wasn't unreasonable. Traveling with a vampire made her mobile and allowed her to call from a remote pay phone without leaving a trace. But what if something happened and she could not call for a month or two or…ever again? Her mum would sit at home and worry herself sick. A clean break would free both of them. "No. I don't wish for you to spend your life waiting by the phone."

Her mother sobbed uncontrollably. "How do you expect me to live if I don't even know you're alive and well?"

Lilah hugged her. "Trust in me, I'll be fine. I know what I'm doing."

"Don't leave me all alone."

Her heart broke at her mother's words, but she had to see this through. "You're not alone, Mum. I need to live my own life, just like you live yours. You've got a great guy by your side now, don't you?" Her mother was still dating Timo, and they had talked about moving in together. Lilah met him a couple of times in the past few months. He was solid as a rock in troubled waters, which was what her mother needed.

"I do, but you're my daughter!"

"And I'll always be your daughter. I love you, and I wish you all the happiness in the world, but I need to do what's best for me. My decision is not up for discussion."

"I won't let you go." Her mum grabbed onto her arm.

She gaped at her mother's fingernails digging into her skin. "You're being ridiculous."

"I don't care. I love you, which is why I can't let you leave."

She clenched her fists. *I'm so sorry, but…I have to do this.* She rose in a swift motion and wrested her arm free with superhuman force. "You can't keep me here. And this is the last time we're here together, so please…let's not part in anger."

Her mother gulped. "You know I'll always love you, honey. Please be careful. I still hope you'll change your mind one day…"

"I know. Take care of yourself." Lilah gave her a kiss. "Goodbye, Mum."

She strode to the front door without looking back.

Chapter 19

Lilah took the next bus to the central railway station and rode a train to Hamburg. With less than four weeks until Christmas, the streets buzzed with people. Thanks to her assignment with Cain at the beginning of the year, she knew vampires frequented the city. Searching for them in the pre-Christmas crowds still felt like looking for the proverbial needle in a haystack.

A vast number of people—all of them human—passed by as she meandered through the city center. Eventually, she picked up on a faint supernatural energy, which guided her to one of the city's Christmas markets. Hundreds of small wooden huts adorned with millions of tiny lights offered roasted almonds, waffles, *poffertjes*, battered fish, and other goodies. Since her stomach growled at the appetizing smells in the air, she had potato pancakes with applesauce for dinner.

She thought about the last time she'd visited a Christmas market. About a year ago, Cain took her on a date to the one in Berlin, treating her to cruller and mulled wine. They enjoyed a romantic ride on a gigantic Ferris wheel. Although they could admire the most amazing view of the bright city lights from within the gondola, he'd only had eyes for her. What was he looking at tonight?

After her meal, she discovered the source of the supernatural energy. Two female vampires were chilling at a booth next to a mulled wine stall. They dressed to kill, and their combination of high boots, deep cleavage, and miniskirt was inappropriate for this time of year. She observed them from a distance while "Last Christmas" blared at her from one of the other stalls.

After a few minutes, a man found his way to the vampires' booth. They invited him to their table and flirted for a while before they both fed on him, masking the act as a make-out session. Eventually, he slumped onto the table as if he'd had too much to drink. Once he regained his senses, they sent him packing and waited for the next guy to repeat the process. Since they didn't even notice a human watching them for almost an hour, she didn't bother to approach them, although she applauded their method of attracting donors.

Her journey took her from Hamburg to Berlin and from there to other big European cities: Prague, Vienna, Budapest, Bucharest, Sofia, Belgrade, Zagreb, Ljubljana, Venice, Munich, Frankfurt, Brussels, and Amsterdam. She avoided Rome so as not to run into Cain. Most of the time, she traveled by day while sleeping on a bus or train to save the cost of accommodations, and she never spent more than two or three nights in the same city. Even though she visited many impressive and historically significant places, she didn't pay attention to the sights, since the search for vampires occupied her mind.

She stumbled across vampires in every city, but most of them didn't notice her, because she was human. Some did, and a few were stupid enough to pick a fight. She scared them off without much effort. None of them were a match for her, so they were of no use to her.

****

After another long journey by coach bus and ferry, Lilah arrived in London—her last hope before giving up on her unfocused search and seeking out Lucious, the only vampire with any power to speak of whom she could link to a city. She dropped her belongings off at a hostel, went to a local pub, and ordered a plate of fish-and-chips with an ale draft beer.

A young vampire entered the pub and pulled up a stool next to her. He looked scarcely twenty years old, with short, spiky blond hair and sapphire-blue eyes. His ripped leather clothes reminded her of an '80s punk. When he noticed her eyes on him, he chatted her up. "All right? My name's Kevin, what's yours?"

She stifled a laugh. "Kevin? Kevin is your actual name?"

"Yea? What's wrong with Kevin?"

"Sorry." She chuckled. "It's just…A vampire called Kevin…You have to admit, it's kinda funny…and sad. Who wants to spend eternity with such a name?"

He gaped at her.

"Oops." She put her hand over her mouth. "Did I say the V-word out loud? Don't worry. I know what you are, but I'm not a hunter. I'm up for a chat if you are."

"If you know what I am, why aren't you afraid of me, lass?"

She shot him an irritated look. "Just because I look like a weak human girl doesn't mean I am one. I can take good care of myself, so don't bother trying anything. If you behave, I'm sure we can both profit from this encounter."

A seductive smile spread across Kevin's lips. "Now, what could you want from me, luv?"

She rolled her eyes. "Not what you're thinking. I'm

looking for information and possibly some of your blood. You can have a taste of mine in return."

He pouted. "Bugger. Why should I give you anything for your blood if I can simply take it?"

"Because you can't." Faster than he could react, she pulled out her dagger and held it to his throat while fixing him with her left arm.

"Blimey, what just happened?"

With a smile, she put the dagger back to the belt around her waist, hiding it beneath her clothes before anyone noticed. "I told you not to try anything. Do I have your attention now?"

He nodded slowly.

"Very well," she said. "Do you know any powerful vampires? The kind who are a few hundred years old and capable of fighting on a high level."

"Why are you looking for powerful vampires?"

"Because I yearn to become stronger. You've already seen a glimpse of my abilities, but they're not enough. I need help to surpass my limits."

"Why do you yearn to become stronger? Are you sure a vampire can help you, then?"

"My reasons are personal, and I'm sure. A vampire helped me surpass human limits before. Anyway, do you know any prominent vampires or not?"

"You're bonkers. I like it." He grinned. "We're a small community here in London. The oldest bloke I know is my sire, but he isn't much older than a century."

Kevin's words confirmed Lilah's fears, although a hundred-year-old vampire wasn't necessarily weak.

"What does your sire do? Is he a fighter?"

He snorted. "Definitely not. He's the lead singer of our punk band."

She burst out laughing. *How audacious!* Because of exposure, a career in performing arts was a dangerous occupation for a vampire. After singing in a band for decades, someone might notice he wasn't aging. Luckily, their recklessness was someone else's problem to deal with.

"Thanks, Kevin. I guess I won't find what I'm looking for here. I appreciate your help, though."

"Chuffed. Didn't you mention an exchange of blood?"

"Follow me." Her gut tightened as she led him out of the pub and to an empty alley. She was out of options, so replenishing the vampire blood in her system was crucial. However, letting a vampire feed on her put her at his mercy. She needed to set up some ground rules. "You may only drink from my wrist. Don't take too much, and don't even consider poisoning me or anything. Otherwise, I'll put a dagger in your heart before you can react." *Please don't call my bluff.* "Numbing the pain would be nice, too."

"You've got a lot of rules."

She shrugged. "I'm simply looking out for myself."

"Got it."

When she offered him her left wrist, he brought it to his mouth and sank his teeth into her flesh without hurting her. He moaned with pleasure when her blood flowed into his mouth. After several pulls, she told him to stop, and he obeyed. He even healed his bite marks.

"I taste power in your blood..." He gawked at her with wide eyes. "Thank you."

"I'm glad you enjoyed it. Now it's my turn."

He tilted his head. "You're serious, then?"

When she nodded, he bit into his wrist and offered

it to her. She sucked on the wound until it stopped bleeding. The quality of his blood differed from Cain's, but after months of not feeding on any vampire, it was better than nothing.

"Blimey, a blood-drinking human…Now I've seen everything."

She chuckled. "Thank you for your blood and for saving me some time here."

Kevin took a bow. "My pleasure."

Chapter 20

A chill crept into Lilah's bones on her ride on the Eurostar to Paris, and it had nothing to do with the cold temperatures in January. Her sense of survival screamed at her to stay away from Lucious, but with no other options, she didn't have the luxury of playing it safe any longer.

The sun still shone when the high-speed train arrived in the City of Love, giving her time to prepare. She walked along the banks of the Seine until she came to the Jardin des Plantes, a botanical garden. The large grounds offered hiding places, wide lawns for fighting, and seclusion from unsuspecting humans after dark. She just had to stay past the opening hours and hide until all staff left.

Once she was all alone, she let her supernatural energy, built through months of feeding on Cain's blood, flow. Cain had taught her not to let any of her telltale power slip so vampires wouldn't consider her a threat or even notice her. She discarded this precaution to fool Lucious into believing a young vampire trespassed into his territory. Attracting his attention was risky but faster than searching the entire city for him.

Dark clouds shrouded the moon on this starless night as she waited, perched on the edge of a bench for hours. When the temperature dropped and snowflakes floated to the ground, she paced around the garden to stay warm. Should she call it a night and look for a hot meal and a safe place to sleep? Her grumbling stomach agreed with the idea. Just then, she felt a change in the air, and her skin crawled. She recognized Lucious' unpleasant aura at once. *Food will have to wait.*

Going down on one knee and bowing her head, she greeted him. "Hello, Lucious."

He appeared right in front of her, wearing a black-and-white tuxedo beneath a black fur cloak. "Well, well, well. What's Cain's pet doing here all alone?"

"I'm not his pet," she bit out. Then, she added in a whisper, "Not anymore."

Lucious focused his gaze on her. "Not anymore? What happened? Trouble in paradise?"

"The asshole abandoned me." Her chest tightened. Calling Cain names felt wrong. Although she hated being separated from him, she understood his reasoning—even if she didn't agree. But right now, she needed Lucious to sympathize with her.

"He did?" Lucious narrowed his eyes. "Then what are you doing in my city? Don't tell me you were looking for me."

She met his icy gaze. "I was."

"Why'd Cain's *former* pet seek me out?"

She lowered her head to hide the contempt on her face. "Because you're the prince of all vampires. You're powerful, and I'm here to ask you to share your power with me."

Lucious snorted. "Why should I share my power with you? You're human. Weak, pathetic, and not worthy of my time."

She bit her lip. "I beg you. Please listen to my proposal. If it's not to your liking, I won't bother you anymore."

"Well, talk. You better not waste my time, or it'll be the last thing you do."

Ignoring the underlying threat, she nodded. "While I lived with Cain, he trained me up to the point where I could subdue a mediocre vampire. I wish to become even stronger—strong enough to best Cain to pay him back for abandoning me. But I can't do it on my own. I need powerful vampires training me and feeding me their blood. You're one of the most powerful vampires I know, so I came to you for help."

"And why would I help you? What's in it for me?"

"I can offer my blood. I'm also willing to serve you or run errands for you."

"Why would I give you anything in exchange for your blood? Cain doesn't care about you anymore, so what keeps me from putting you into a cell in my dungeon?"

She gulped. She had to be careful how she handled him. Did her strength suffice to subdue him if it came to a fight? "Nothing…But where is the fun in me rotting in one of your dungeons? Cain won't care. He doesn't even know where I am or what I'm doing. If you helped me and I won in a fight against him, I'd degrade him."

"Tempting." Lucious' smile froze the blood in her veins. "But what if I don't believe you'd ever stand a chance against him? What if I'm convinced he still cares about you? And what if I killed you now to throw it in his face later?"

Cain would kill you. Since this knowledge wouldn't save her from him, she needed to handle the situation on her own and bet everything on her power. A sense of calm overcame her as she gazed directly into his light-blue eyes. "How about I show you what I can do? Fight me. Whoever lands the first hit wins. If you win, you can do with me as you please. If I can't even land a hit on you, I'll never win against Cain, and my life loses its meaning. However, if I win, you'll train me and feed me your blood. What do you say?"

Lucious drew his sword with a smirk. "You have a deal."

A deal with the devil.

With her chain whip in hand, she crouched down like an animal. When Lucious tried to sever her right arm with a strike of his sword, she jumped to her feet to avoid his attack, spun around, and used the momentum to lash at him.

He underestimated her speed, and her whip grazed his leg before he put enough distance between them. Lucious gaped at her, flabbergasted. He opened his mouth, but words eluded him.

She hadn't expected to land a hit with so little effort. She kneeled down to show respect and to put her victory into perspective since she needed him to believe she was no threat. "The element of surprise is usually on my side, and I needed nothing else. I'm not fooling myself. I probably won't land another hit, because you know now what you're dealing with."

"Wise words. Maybe you're not completely useless. Since I'm in a good mood today, I'll assist you."

"Thank you." With careful treading and luck, she'd get out of their alliance alive and stronger than ever.

"What kind of training are you looking for?" he asked.

"Combat training is always helpful. And from what I've heard, your true strength lies in concealment and observation. I want you to teach those skills to me."

"How will observation skills help you defeat Cain?"

"They'll help me survive in the long run. I'm human, so learning from one formidable vampire won't bring me to Cain's level. Training with you is step one of many. The bottom line is, I need several powerful vampires to support me. If every one of them taught me their best skills, I might stand a chance against Cain. What do you think?"

"Your plan might work…However, if you amass so much power, I hope you won't ever forget who helped you," Lucious warned her. He obviously didn't want to raise himself another dangerous foe like Cain.

She didn't intend to make enemies. "I won't forget, and I'll never turn on those who help me," she promised.

"Okay, then, come with me."

****

Lucious owned a beautiful mansion on the outskirts of Paris. Compared to the king's castle or Cain's house, his private residence was quite modern. With designer furniture, a heated pool in the garden, bright colors, and big window fronts, no one would expect a cruel and vindictive vampire lived there.

"You look surprised," he noted after giving her a tour. "Were you expecting another dungeon?"

"As a matter of fact, I was," she said.

Lucious' stylish living room comprised a massive black leather couch, a white table, white cupboards, and a big, white entertainment center with a huge plasma TV. While he luxuriated on the couch, she showed him respect by kneeling on the floor with her head bowed.

"You won't find one here," he said. "This house is for light fun only. I use it for pool parties and other high-society events. There are solely humans on the guest list, which gives me an almost endless buffet of spoiled, well-fed nouveau riche.

"It's a hobby I don't share with other vampires of the court, which makes this the ideal place to keep you hidden from prying eyes. In this context, I'd prefer our little arrangement to stay between us."

"I understand."

"Very well. Apart from a daily cleaning service, you'll be the only one here. The fridge is always stocked, and you can use the pool and the fitness room to stay in shape. The grounds are wide enough to train without attracting my neighbors' attention. I'll drop by whenever I can detach myself from court."

"Thank you. I'll eagerly await our training sessions. What about feeding me your blood regularly to build up my strength?"

"How often is regularly? I'm in high demand, so I can't afford to drop by daily. I'll try to fit you into my busy schedule, though...Which reminds me, you promised me your blood, and I am peckish after so much talking."

An icy shudder swept through her body. Her blood was the only thing she could offer to a vampire.

Images of the first time he'd fed from her flashed in front of her eyes, freezing her to the spot. There was no time like the present to get over a trauma, though. Since she depended on his help, she had to trust him not to take advantage of her in a vulnerable position. She took a deep breath, walked over to him, and offered her wrist.

"Don't insult me," he said derisively.

"Sorry," she mumbled. Her body shook as she sat on the couch, pulled her hair to one side, and tilted her head to bare her throat.

"Much better." He leaned close and took a whiff of her sensitive skin.

She shivered, plagued by memories of him torturing her.

When he bit down, she clenched her jaw so as not to cry out. He didn't bother numbing the pain, and her body quaked in agony. But she wouldn't grant him the satisfaction of seeing how much he hurt her, so she shut her eyes to keep the tears from falling.

After an excruciating minute, he released her. Unlike the last time he'd taken her blood, he closed off the bite marks.

"Why do you enjoy hurting others?" The words slipped out of her mouth.

"Why? Did I hurt you?" Lucious feigned surprise.

"You know you did, but I'm not complaining. If it means getting closer to my goal, I can endure pain. I'm merely wondering if there's a reason."

"I inflict pain because I can. Why should I, the prince of all vampires, care about other people's feelings?"

He had a point, and in a twisted way, she could relate. She hadn't gotten along with her classmates in middle school, because she hadn't cared about anyone's opinion. Who was she to tell an over-four-hundred-year-old vampire he'd end up lonely with his way of living? As prince, chances were he wouldn't. She shrugged.

"You also asked for my blood, and you shall get it. I hope you appreciate being one of the few people to taste my power." He cut into his wrist with a sharp fingernail and offered it to her. His eyes widened when she lowered her head to drink from his bleeding wrist. "I've never seen a human consume blood by choice."

"I don't enjoy the taste like you do, and it takes a lot of willpower not to retch. But I appreciate the power in your blood because it strengthens me. Thank you."

He nodded curtly before leaving her on her own.

Once he vanished, she melted onto the couch. Traveling through Europe for weeks, without a place to return to, wore her out. She relished having a beautiful mansion to herself after sleeping in buses or sharing hostel rooms with strangers.

****

Lilah was enjoying a swim when her gaze fell on Lucious standing at the edge of the pool. Her heart rocketed in her chest as she got out of the water and kneeled in front of him. Where had he suddenly appeared from? His aura usually warned her of his presence, but there was nothing, not even the slightest tingle in the air. Yet he stood right there. "How come I don't feel your aura?"

"So you can recognize a vampire's aura? Fascinating."

The moment he spoke these words, his presence hit her with full force, causing her hair to stand on end. Or was it the cool air around her? She nodded.

"To answer your question, I concealed my aura from you. You wished to learn about concealment techniques, didn't you?"

"Yes, please," she said. "How does it work?"

"It's simple, really. Calm your mind and cease your breathing to slow your heartbeat."

"Cease my breathing?" She blinked a few times. "You know humans need to breathe, right?"

He shrugged. "What a pity for you."

Is he kidding me? "Do you have any other advice for me?"

"Not really…there's not much else to it. If you absolutely must breathe, at least slow your breathing. It might suffice since you're human and have a good grasp of your superhuman energy."

"All right…thanks." She sighed inwardly.

In addition to being a useless teacher, Lucious was also a poor training partner. As his fighting style was rather simplistic and blunt, she quickly got the hang of it. After a few sessions, she could foresee and react to every one of his moves. She was careful not to defeat him during their training, though. Hurting his fragile ego only led to a more painful experience when he fed on her.

His royal blood alone kept her at his house. It was more potent than Cain's, and every time she drank from his veins, her power grew.

Chapter 21

Once spring brought new life to the world around her, the urge to move on sprouted in Lilah.

"I'd like a quick word if you please," she addressed Lucious after drinking his blood.

"I'm listening."

She kneeled and bowed her head. "As I've told you in the beginning, I aspire to learn from different vampires. I think now is a good time to move on. If possible, I'd like to leave with your blessing and a recommendation where to go."

Lucious studied her. "If you think it's best for you to continue your training elsewhere, I won't stop you. I wonder where your journey will lead you...My father is right. You'd make an interesting vampire."

"How did you know?"

"Know what? That you're trying to become stronger because Cain would only turn you if you beat him?"

Her mouth fell open. If he already knew, there was no denying it, so she nodded.

He laughed. "You just told me. I had my suspicions—nothing eludes my grasp. My father mentioned your visit to court, and Cain was even grumpier than usual when I encountered him soon after. I'm curious to witness the effect you'll have on him if you succeed."

She felt a twinge in her chest at the news about Cain.

How was he dealing without her? Would her path lead back to him in the end?

"Well, since we're on the same page, do you have any suggestions where I could go next?" she asked again.

"If you're looking for fighting experience, the fight club might be a good place to start."

"Fight club?"

"It's a small clan of vampires who spend too much time fighting each other for fun. Most of them aren't strong, but there are exceptions."

"Sounds fun!"

"And dangerous or even deadly for a human," he noted.

She shrugged. "If I cared about my safety, I wouldn't have come here. Where can I find them?"

"From what I've heard, they reside somewhere in Dublin. Since most of them don't care for royalty, I've never been to their hideout. But it should be easy to find—just look for the place where the vampires gather...Good luck."

With a smirk on his lips, he teleported away.

"If I knew where they gathered, I wouldn't have asked for your help in the first place," she muttered to herself.

After packing her backpack, she took a bus to London and another one from there to Dublin.

On the ride, she remembered her last visit to Ireland. She and Cain had spent the night in an Irish pub, listening to live music. Several musicians performed a mix of different genres, ranging from traditional folk music over rock songs to romantic ballads. During the quieter pieces, he pulled her onto his lap, wrapping his arms around her waist. Her heart danced as she cuddled against him. She'd loved his proximity and the way his heady scent enveloped her.

****

Once she arrived in Dublin city center, she concentrated on supernatural auras in her vicinity. A clot of energy not too far from her location stood out, suggesting at least a handful of vampires. Although none of them felt particularly strong, they were her best bet.

After a twenty-minute walk, she arrived at a vast, abandoned warehouse. Not even a dozen streetlamps illuminated the neighborhood. The surrounding buildings were decaying, and graffiti decorated most walls. Dull sounds came from within the warehouse.

She suppressed her energy and sneaked through a broken window. Hundreds of empty paper boxes greeted her, and she stowed her backpack in one of them. A faint light led her farther into the building. After passing through two doors, she reached a long hallway leading to a badly illuminated room, filled with fighting sounds and cheering noises. She edged closer and stopped next to the open door to glimpse what was going on without being seen herself.

Various boxes filled most of the room except for a large area in the middle. Two bare-chested vampires occupied the space, caught in a bloody boxing match. Five more vampires had spread through the room and watched them. Four of the onlookers cheered, whereas the fifth sat nonchalantly on a wooden box.

While the two boxers held the attention of the other vampires, she sneaked into the room and hid behind a box to get a closer look at their fighting style.

The match was about to end. One of the fighters, a bulky, bald-headed guy, dominated the fight. His opponent, a slim, black-haired vampire with a hooked nose, couldn't evade his powerful punches any longer. When the bulky one delivered a forceful blow to the guts, the slim one doubled over and slumped to the ground. A final cheer greeted the winner.

"Who wants to go next?" he shouted after kicking his opponent a few times.

The cheering stopped.

"You cowards," he taunted them to no avail before turning to the guy on the box. "How about you, Laurant?"

"You don't want to fight me," Laurant warned. He had short, blond hair, hazel eyes, and wore a gray suit.

"I'll get you down eventually," the baldhead promised.

"We'll see." Laurant turned his head in Lilah's direction. "Maybe our uninvited guest would like to give it a go?"

All heads turned to Lilah, and her heart sank to her knees.

"Shit." She hadn't planned on facing them right away, but he left her no choice. Taking a dagger in each hand, she jumped in front of the box she'd been hiding behind. "I'm impressed you noticed me."

Laurant eyed her. "I'm not sure if you impress or amuse me, hunter. Coming here on your own—you're courageous."

"Oh please, I'm no hunter," she complained.

"Then what are you, a human equipped with silver weapons, doing here?"

"I'm looking for fighting experience and vampire blood to boost my power, so I'll accept the challenge." She fixed her gaze on the bald vampire.

A huge smile crept across his face. "Dinner came to me tonight."

"Don't get your hopes up too soon," she cautioned him. "Are there any rules?"

"No, there are none. It's a one-on-one fight. Just try not to get yourself killed too quickly." Laurant chuckled.

"I won't." She walked to the center of the room while keeping her eyes on the baldhead. The humming and flickering of the ceiling lamp wracked her nerves.

Every vampire in the room gawked at her, but she didn't care. Laurant said they fought one-on-one, so she only had to concern herself with one of them. After seeing his first match, she wouldn't underestimate her opponent. She closed her eyes for a moment, breathed in, and let her instincts take over.

"Are you scared to look fate in the eye?" the baldhead asked.

"You don't scare me." She smirked at him. "Are you scared? If not, come and get me!"

He threw himself at her, but she sidestepped him. With an angry snort, he turned around and tried again and again. Yet she didn't let him touch her. Except for Laurant, all vampires laughed, which infuriated the baldhead even more.

"What are you?" he growled.

"I'm human."

"No human is this fast."

"A vampire taught me how to fight and protect myself. Anything is possible if you try hard."

"Bullshit. You're fast, but you'll never win by running away. Once you tire, you'll be mine."

She didn't evade the baldhead's next punch. Instead, she blocked his fist with her left hand while using her right one to slash her dagger at him. He fended her blade off with his left arm, but the silver still cut into his flesh. Cursing, he put some distance between them. The onlookers cheered for her.

She licked his blood off her dagger. "Don't make assumptions. Just because I gave you the chance to come at me first doesn't mean I can't strike back."

He came at her with more force, trying to land one hit after another for almost ten minutes. Even though she blocked most punches, the force he put into them took their toll and slowed down her movements.

"Not so powerful now, are we?" the baldhead mocked her.

She gritted her teeth. Since he didn't underestimate her any longer, she'd lost her advantage. Unlike her, he wouldn't tire, which forced her to change tactics. The next time he attacked, she didn't dodge or block. The impact of his fist on her ribs sent a searing pain through her body, but she ignored it long enough to ram her dagger into his stomach.

They both doubled over in pain. She pulled herself together faster than he did. After all the times Lucious had fed on her, pain didn't faze her. She threw herself at baldhead and kept him pinned to the floor while pressing her second dagger to his throat. When he tried to shove her off, the blade cut into his flesh, and he winced.

"Are you giving up?" she asked.

"All right," he grunted.

She got up, removed her other dagger from his stomach, and licked the blade clean. "Your blood isn't too bad."

A chuckle sounded from behind. "After putting on a show for us, tell me, what do you really want?"

She turned around to face Laurant. "Opportunities to become stronger. I'll take whatever I can get. You enjoy a good fight, so I'm sure we can work something out here?"

"Intriguing," he said. "I'll take you under my wing if you're interested."

Even though he called the shots, Laurant didn't feel powerful. Was he hiding his true strength?

"Depends. I haven't seen you fight yet."

"Only willing to learn from the best, are you?" He grinned. "I understand. However, I doubt you're up for another fight tonight, and none of the vampires here are worth the effort. So take my word for it. Since the sun will rise soon, you better decide now."

"Okay, I'm in."

Chapter 22

Laurant lived in the penthouse of a high-rise building. He showed Lilah around, and the tour ended on his rooftop terrace, which offered an incredible view of Dublin. From the edge of the roof, she gazed into the distance and watched the sky turn red.

"Do you frequently go home with vampires you don't know?"

"Hilarious," she replied dryly. "As you've seen, I can protect myself. Finding strong vampires isn't easy, so I can't let this chance pass me by."

"May I ask why you long to become stronger?"

"I need to win a fight against someone. Since he's one of the strongest vampires alive, it'll be a tough challenge."

"Someone? Who are you talking about? And why do you have to beat him?"

"Sorry, I can't tell you more," she said. "With vampire politics, alliances, and feuds, I'd rather keep any information regarding the vampires I've met confidential. I don't wish to cause any trouble."

"What a pity. I fancy juicy stories, but I get your point. Since I also don't like other vampires knowing too much about my life, I appreciate your confidentiality. What's your name? Or is it confidential as well?"

"No, it's not." She chuckled. "I'm Lilah. Nice to meet you."

"I'm Laurant. How did you find us?"

She dropped her gaze to the floor. "Someone told me about a fight club in Dublin."

"Not much information there, either." He turned away from her with a sigh. "Since the sky is becoming lighter by the minute, I'll go to sleep. You can stay in the guest room, and we can discuss everything else when I get up."

"So you're sleeping right here with a human running around your flat?"

"Why not?" Laurant chuckled. "Should I worry about you assaulting me while I sleep?"

"Of course not. I'm just surprised. The vampires I've met so far were more secretive about where they slept." Cain had never revealed the exact location of his private bedroom, and Lucious had slept somewhere else altogether.

"I'm confident I can defend myself, so there's no need to hide. Good night."

She still watched the sunrise for a while, wishing she could watch it with Cain.

****

The next evening, Lilah found Laurant in front of a hallway mirror, fixing his tie.

"You're up early." She eyed his appearance. "Fancy. Do you always dress in a suit?"

"Yes, as a matter of course, I wear a suit at my job. Speaking of which, something's come up at work, so I don't have time for you this evening."

"Where do you work?"

"I'm the CEO of an IT company downtown."

She stared at him for a moment before finding her voice. "IT? Seriously?"

"Yes. I enjoy staying connected to the human world and up-to-date with their innovations. It's entertaining to observe how humans live, what they deal with, and how they experience their life. Anyway, I need to get going."

"Can I join you?"

He examined her from head to toe. "No. You're not dressed appropriately."

"Not dressed appropriately?" She glanced at her black jeans and sweater. "I'm not going for a job interview or anything. My outfit is plain and inconspicuous, so you can't say it's inappropriate. Come on, please?"

He sighed. "All right, follow me."

They took an elevator down to the building's underground parking lot. Her eyes bulged when he got into a black, low-slung sports car.

"Don't just stand there." He chuckled. "I've got a meeting in half an hour."

The motor roared as she plummeted onto the soft leather seat.

Fifteen minutes later, he parked the car in front of a tall building with a glass front. They took an elevator to the top floor, where a middle-aged woman with short, brown hair greeted them.

"Good evening, Laurant. I've already prepared everything in your office. Who's the young lady?"

"Evening, Susan. This is Lilah, a…cousin from abroad."

Lilah smiled at her. "Hello, nice to meet you."

Susan returned the smile. "Likewise. Can I get you anything? A coffee, maybe?"

"Sure, thank you."

"The usual for you, Laurant?" Susan asked.

"Yes, thank you," he said and motioned to Lilah to follow him.

His office consisted of a massive desk with a laptop, shelves filled with folders and technology books, and a lounge facing the glass outer wall. Over a dozen vitrines displayed technical drawings and various inventions, including an astrolabe, a mechanical clock, and an engine.

She didn't know half the names of the other items. "What are those?"

"Collectibles I picked up throughout the ages," he said while sorting through a pile of files.

She spotted a sketch by Leonardo da Vinci. Was it genuine?

"Did you actually meet—" She swallowed the rest of her question when Susan entered with a cup of coffee for her and an espresso for Laurant.

"Your client is already waiting in meeting room three," Susan said.

"Thank you." He took a sip of the espresso before getting to his feet. "Will you be okay waiting here for a while?" he asked Lilah.

"Of course."

While Laurant took care of his business, she made herself comfortable in a lounge chair. The view of the downtown lights from high above stole her breath.

****

"I'm done for tonight," Laurant announced over two hours later. "Now, are you up for some exercise? I still owe you a demonstration of my powers."

"Sure!"

He teleported both of them back to the old warehouse. With no other vampires around, they had the building to themselves.

"Come at me if you're ready," he challenged her.

She eyed his suit warily. "Shouldn't you put on something more...appropriate for battle?"

"Why? Don't worry about ripping my clothes or anything. There are hundreds of suits where this one came from. It's my usual attire for fighting."

"All right." With one swift move, she pulled her whip out of her pocket and slashed at him, but he evaded her hit.

"It won't be easy to rip my suit. You better try harder," he mocked her.

She tried again and failed. He moved too fast for her to see.

"Impressive," she said. "You're much faster than I gave you credit for. What else you got?"

When he switched to the offense, she let her whip drop and drew her daggers to fend him off. She blocked his first hit. His second hit caused her to loosen her grip on one of her daggers, which fell to the floor with a clank. The third one landed on her ribs.

"Damn it," she hissed and jumped back. He fought exceedingly well.

"Giving up already?" he asked with a smile on his lips.

"Never!"

She charged at him. Since her blades had lost their value in a fight against him, she repurposed her remaining dagger as a throwing weapon aimed at his head. He evaded her attack, which was nothing but a diversion. While he focused on the dagger, she got close enough to tackle him to the ground. She intended to limit his movements, but he reacted much faster than she did.

He turned around, rolled her onto her back, and pinned her down.

"Not bad. As you can see, there's no need for you to worry about ripping my suit."

She pouted. Who'd expect a vampire dressed in a suit to fight well? "I admit I've underestimated you. If you want my blood, go ahead, you've earned it." She offered him her neck.

He shook his head and let her go. "You're brave, but I don't crave blood now. Maybe I'll come back to your offer later on. I don't feed on humans often."

"You don't? How old are you?" She sat up and studied him.

"I'm tempted to say my age is confidential," he said with a twinkle in his eyes. "But I won't, because knowing my age will impart an estimate of my strength and experience to you. I'm almost eight hundred years old."

She gulped. "Don't take it the wrong way, but you seem much younger."

"Staying in touch with humans keeps me young. I live my life to the fullest, and I don't show off my strength. Even when I enjoy a brawl at the fight club, I hold back because I don't wish to discourage my opponents before they face me."

"Huh, clever. Truth be told, I'd have hesitated to attack you if I'd known your age."

"I'm glad you didn't. You show promise, and I'd be happy to train you." Something gleamed in his eyes.

"Thanks! So…even if you don't crave my blood now, can I get some of yours?"

"Licking the blood off the blade last night wasn't for show?"

She grinned. "Nope. Drinking blood is disgusting, but with every dose I ingest, my senses heighten, my strength grows, and training becomes more efficient. Since the effect correlates with a vampire's age and power, I'm curious how your blood will affect me if you let me have some."

"Sure. I want to see you reach your full potential after all."

"Why are you so invested in helping me?" She furrowed her brows.

"Nothing is more exhilarating than a good battle. If I can assist you *and* get an entertaining sparring partner, it's a win-win."

Chapter 23

Every time Lilah took a sip of Laurant's highly potent blood, she felt as if she absorbed part of his long-life experiences. In contrast to Cain, who'd taught her to fight as a means to defend herself, Laurant enjoyed every minute of the endless hours they spent fighting and discovering their physical and mental limits.

She started most nights with a jog through the city while Laurant attended to his business. Afterward, they met up in the abandoned warehouse and fought each other for the better part of the night. As he specialized in fighting weaponless and had disarmed her countless times, she gave up on weapons. They put her at a disadvantage because losing and retrieving them drew her concentration away from him.

Sometimes, other members joined them. According to Laurant, the fight club was an international association of vampires who enjoyed a good brawl. Most fighters were less than a century old and not very powerful, though.

He encouraged whoever showed up to compete with her. He watched the battles and commented on her fighting style and possibilities for improvement.

On a hot summer night, he took his comments to a new level. She was up against twins from Sweden. The two vampires not only looked alike, but they also synced their movements perfectly. After parrying an almost endless string of attacks, she brought both of them down at the same time with a roundhouse kick.

When she turned to Laurant, he shuffled through a pile of papers before deciding on a sheet with a large five on it. "Five points for your endurance. Your movements slowed down toward the end of the fight." He held up the next sheet, an eight. "Eight for your defense. Even though they came at you from two sides, you parried everything." The final number was a seven. "And seven points for your offense. Your attacks lacked vigor."

"Um…what are you doing?" She stared at him.

"I watched a casting show a few days ago…The rating process seemed fun, so I wanted to try it."

The concept cracked her up. Once she calmed down, she asked, "When do you even have time to watch TV in between training with me and running your business?"

"I multitask." He grinned. "Besides, it's a great way to track your progress."

****

Rumors about a human triumphing in the fight club spread among its members and attracted more vampires who challenged her, giving her the opportunity to refine her fighting skills in battles against opponents from all over Europe. After half a year of training, she felt ready to take on almost anyone.

Laurant still had the upper hand whenever they fought, but since he had nearly eight hundred years on her and she already had him sweating, she took it as a win.

A three-hundred-year-old Greek vampire called Damian broke her confidence. With his average height, dark hair, and brown eyes, he looked ordinary, but his fighting style set him apart.

Unlike most of the fight club members, he used a weapon. Just as Laurant had taught her, she wanted to start the fight against Damian by disarming him. Unfortunately, he was a master of stick fighting. With a delicately carved wooden staff, he kept her at a distance and blocked each of her attempts to weaken his hold on the weapon. For two hours, she attacked him relentlessly, hoping to knock the staff out of his hand, but he parried her onslaught.

Eventually, Laurant offered some advice from the sidelines. "If your opponent doesn't let you get close, you must adapt. Try switching to a weapon with a similar distance."

She groaned. Her only long-range weapon was a chain whip she hadn't used in months. She always carried it coiled up in her pants pocket, though. To avoid the imminent loss due to exhaustion, changing tactics was her best option.

Damian eyed her whip warily, but he didn't comment. He hadn't spoken at all during their fight.

Even with her whip, the tide didn't turn for her. Damian deflected each slash with his staff. When she wrapped the end of her whip around his weapon to disarm him, her plan backfired. His grip on the staff was too strong, and he disarmed her with a calculated, vigorous pull. The moment her weapon fell to the floor, she knew she'd never win.

"I surrender," she announced, raising her hands in defeat. "Without a similar weapon and proficiency, I'll never gain the upper hand. We could go on for hours, but I'll tire before you do, so let's end it here."

"It's not your style to capitulate. In fact, I've never seen you quit before," Laurant noted.

She shrugged and turned to face Damian, whose grim face and slumped posture conveyed the impression he'd lost the match.

"Don't look so glum," she said. "I'd have lost either way, so you may feed on me."

"I'd prefer a decent match," Damian said.

"Well, I'm always up for a rematch, but unless I gain some serious experience in fighting with weapons, I can't offer you a good one. How about you teach me?" she asked, sniffing a chance. Even though her time with Laurant was fruitful, her progress had stagnated lately.

"Why should I waste my time on you?"

Heat flushed through her body and her nostrils flared at his biased question, but she took a calming breath before arguing her case. "It's not wasted time. You enjoy a good fight—otherwise you wouldn't be here. With your help, I can offer you a great fight in next to no time."

"I don't—" he started, but Laurant intervened.

"Give her a chance, Damian. I've improved my own skills while helping her, so I'm sure you will, too. Besides, her progress is astounding, and she's fun to hang out with. Even though I'd love for her to stay longer, I know she'd benefit from training with you."

Guilt must have been clear on her face when she turned to Laurant—she should have talked to him first.

Laurant smiled at her. "It's all right."

Damian watched them thoughtfully. "Fine…As long as you're no inconvenience." His eyes narrowed on her. "And I won't take care of you."

"I can take care of myself."

Chapter 24

The sound of breaking waves and the salty smell of the sea filled the air. Hills, cliffs, and low shrubs growing on dry ground shaped the landscape.

"Where are we?" Lilah asked.

"Polyegos, a currently uninhabited Greek island," Damian answered.

Her mouth went dry. *Uninhabited?*

He brought her to a simplistic, white clay hut, with two rooms out of a different time period, on the edge of a steep cliff. The first room combined a living room and a kitchen with an old-looking stove, a cupboard, a huge bucket filled with water, a table with three chairs, and a shelf. The second room contained a bed, a chest, and a small bedside table. There were no bathroom facilities, no running water, and no electricity.

"How do you survive here?" she asked after getting over her initial shock.

Damian shrugged. "I'm a vampire. Since I'm currently not using this house, you can stay here. It's late, so we'll start training tomorrow."

He left without further notice. She became dizzy when the severity of her situation hit her. Where would she find food or fresh drinking water? Taking care of herself suddenly got a whole different meaning. Since panic never helped, she took several long, calming breaths. Surviving on an island wasn't her biggest challenge to date.

As the sun hadn't risen yet, she went on a run to explore her surroundings in the dim light of the moon. The rocky island measured approximately six kilometers in length. Little streams with crystal clear, drinkable water flowed from the top of the hills to the sea. Despite the sparse vegetation, bushes with edible berries and other fruits grew everywhere. Sandy beaches, caves, and the ruins of an old monastery painted the picture of a holiday paradise. A picturesque, white lighthouse stood on the other side of the island, and she spotted two fishermen on a boat close to the coast.

Wild goats and rabbits roamed the island, and she wondered if she could kill an animal to survive. The irony of the question didn't elude her. After all, she was working toward her goal of becoming a creature even further up on the food chain, whose hunger surpassed a human's by far. If she succeeded, no one would spoon-feed her the blood of her victims.

After eating her fill of berries, she returned to the hut shortly before noon and fell asleep on the hard bed.

****

"Why are you still sleeping? Didn't you want to learn something?" Damian's voice woke Lilah.

"I do!" She stifled a yawn and got up.

He tossed her a staff and walked outside. Before following him, she noticed a loaf of bread on the table, and a slow smile built on her lips.

"Show me what you can do with a staff," he prompted her.

She lunged at him, but he blocked her weapon with little effort. When she tried again, his counterattack almost made her lose the grip on her staff.

He shook his head in disappointment. "You're holding it wrong. It's not a sword, you know? I guess we start with the basics."

She sighed. Cain had shown her how to wield a staff, but he primarily used swords. In fact, his corresponding fighting techniques varied little for all the weapons he'd taught her. "All right. What are the basics?"

"The most useful movement is the spinning of your staff." He spun his staff while alternating between his left and right hand. "The faster you spin, the harder it'll be for an enemy to get close to you. At the same time, it's important to keep complete control of your weapon so you don't lose it."

Spinning a staff wasn't as easy as it looked. He watched her attempts with an amused expression.

"It takes a lot of practice. Let me know once you've mastered the movement," he said.

"Wait, please," she said with an urgency when he turned to leave. "I progress much faster with vampire blood in my system. Would you give me some of yours? You can feed on me, too."

He studied her for a moment. "No."

"What?" She gawked at Damian, who vanished without giving her a chance to argue. After a long sigh, she resumed spinning her staff. With the remnants of Laurant's blood in her system, going a few weeks without feeding on a vampire didn't enervate her, but it thwarted her progress.

****

It took Lilah two weeks of constant staff spinning until Damian acknowledged her progress. Her training continued in a similar fashion. He showed her new movements and then left her to practice on her own.

With no one to talk to except for Damian, who was rather quiet and mostly absent, loneliness overcame her. Living in a medieval hut with no electricity and no running water added to her discomfort. After a while, not even the warm rays of the sun around dusk, the sounds of the ocean, or the breathtaking scenery lifted her mood.

Moreover, fall wouldn't last forever. The days grew shorter, and the temperature cooled every day, which gave her another reason to keep her time on the island as short as possible.

After six more weeks, she couldn't stand another minute on the island. She'd mastered the basics of using a staff, and everything else would follow with practice. Before challenging Damian to the promised duel, she feasted on a rabbit.

Hunting for the protein-rich meal had been easy. With supernatural speed, she caught the animal and cut its throat without reflecting too much on it. But her hands trembled as she skinned and gutted the poor creature with her dagger. Its blood spattered her clothes and hands, and the sight made her nauseous. Why did it affect her so much? She washed the blood off in a nearby stream while the meat grilled over an open fire. Once it was well-done, she savored every bite.

Damian came by early the next evening.

She faced him with her staff in hand. "It's time for me to move on, but I still owe you a great fight. Are you prepared to face me now?"

"I doubt you can even offer a *good* fight," he said. "But I never turn down a challenge, so…try to prove me wrong."

"With pleasure." She spun her staff with a smile on her lips, waiting for him to attack.

He came at her, but she fended him off. When he struck again, she put more force into her weapon, blocked, and pushed him back. He nodded approvingly before assaulting her with fast strikes. Somehow, spinning her staff made up for the supernatural speed she lacked and enabled her to parry everything.

The next time he charged at her, she used both of her hands to put power behind her blocking strike. Both staves locked, and she pushed his staff outward. The tip of her weapon was between his staff and his face—a perfect position to strike. She directed her power toward his face, hoping to land a hit. But he let his weapon fall, went down on his hands, and attacked her with a spinning heel kick.

While she jumped back to dodge his counterattack, he regained control of his weapon.

"So you *can* fight without your staff," she said, impressed.

"I prefer not to, but every fighter should have a plan B. You can take pride in forcing me to resort to such measures."

"I will, after bringing you down!"

She attacked with fast, relentless strikes and stabs, but he blocked each of her moves. Was it impossible to beat a staff master with a staff?

Using his spinning heel kick as an inspiration, she contemplated ways to combine her new techniques with Laurant's lessons. In their first match, she hadn't been able to disarm Damian without a decent, long-range weapon. Since she fought with one now, she gave the disarming tactic another shot.

To weaken his firm hold on the weapon, she aimed at his wrist. Even though he fended her off, her powerful strikes took their toll. When he passed his staff from his right to his left hand, she seized her chance and aimed at the space between his hands. His weapon got caught in the spin of hers and dropped to the floor. She tackled him, pushed him to the ground, and pinned him down with her staff across his chest.

"Got you," she panted.

He smiled. "What an interesting fight! You learned fast."

"Thank you!" Since Damian talked little, she appreciated his praise even more. "I like staves. It's a pity they are rather bulky, though. I can't conceal them as easily as a dagger."

They both got to their feet, and he vanished like so many times before. She groaned. Why didn't he ever stay long enough for a decent conversation? She didn't want to spend another night there, but leaving on her own was tricky. Could she draw the local fishermen's attention and convince them to bring her to a populated island?

When she packed up her stuff with the goal of making her way to the lighthouse, he reappeared.

"As a prize for your victory." He offered her a thirty-centimeter-long, silver-coated stick.

She examined the item to discover it was a retractable staff. Her face lit up. "It's perfect, thank you!"

"There's no reason for me to hide my weapon. My sire, also a stick-fighting master, gave it to me, and I carry it with pride. But you benefit from the element of surprise, so I'm sure this concealable staff will come in handy."

"Definitely. Thank you so much!"

"Where will you go next?" he asked.

"I don't know yet. You've seen me fight...What

should I work on? Do you know anyone who's skilled at something I'm lacking?"

He looked her up and down. "You could optimize your movements and the way you present yourself. You probably don't even realize you move differently. A vampire's movements are smooth, whereas yours are jerky and predictable."

"Do you know anyone who could help me work on that?"

His gaze wandered. "Long ago, I met a vampire who founded a circus group. She's encouraged human artists to perfect their movements to mesmerize the audience for a long time. Maybe she can help you." When Lilah frowned, he added, "It's just a suggestion. Besides, I don't know where you can find her. We lost contact several decades ago. As far as I know, she's still traveling through Europe with her circus."

"There's no harm in trying. What's her name? And can you drop me off somewhere close to where she might be?"

He nodded. "Her name is Lexi, although I don't know if she's still going by that name. As she's living among humans, she has to change her identity every other decade. By the way, don't mention my name if you find her."

"Why not? Toxic relationship?" she joked, but he didn't answer. "Don't worry, I'll keep your name and everything else I've learned about you to myself. With so little information, I'm not sure I can find her, anyway. Do you have any other clues, for example, the name of her circus?"

"I don't remember the name. She sticks to Eastern Europe, so try your luck in the Czech Republic, Slovakia,

Hungary, or Romania. Since it's almost winter, her circus won't travel much."

"Well, it's a start." She smiled. "Thanks."

In one night, he'd told her more than in the past eight weeks combined.

Chapter 25

Damian dropped Lilah off in Prague, where colorful placards led her to a huge, yellow-and-red-striped circus tent. The performance finished shortly after her arrival, but she stayed to watch the circus workers clean and take care of the animals. There were no vampires among them.

Next, she stopped at an internet café, where she researched the locations of circus groups in Eastern Europe, wrote a list of over ten possibilities, and booked a bus to the nearest one. She spent the next three weeks traveling through the Czech Republic and Slovakia, where she checked out every circus she could find.

If she arrived in time for the evening performance, she'd watch the show, hoping to spot a vampire. Even though some artists moved in a superhuman way, all were human. The acts were still amazing and illustrated her margin for improvement.

One of her destinations, Bardejov, was close to the village where Cain grew up. Not long after telling her his story, he'd shown her the church where he spent his childhood. The wooden building had survived the centuries, but the colors on the interior walls were fading. According to him, most of the wall paintings hadn't even existed when he lived there.

"After my iniquity, I didn't dare to return." He trailed his hands along the walls and benches, and a shudder went through him. "I never expected to find myself here again."

He sat down in the front row, made the sign of the cross, folded his hands, and prayed for a moment with his eyes closed.

"Why did you bring me here, then?" she asked once he rose.

"I guess I wanted you to know where I come from." He held out his hand.

She took it and let him lead her outside.

After taking a deep breath, he surveyed the area. "Not much has changed…As if God kept it this way to remind me of my sin."

"Or to remind you of happier times when you lived here as a child."

"Maybe." He stared at the ground and cleared his throat. "How about we look for a restaurant for you?"

She'd let him change the topic. Could she have changed anything if she'd insisted on discussing his guilt and feelings back then?

****

Eventually, Lilah crossed the border to Hungary and arrived at a circus on the outskirts of Budapest around dusk. With a bag of salty popcorn with melted butter, she seized a seat in the first row and waited for the show to start. Her heart pounded with excitement when the circus director, a woman dressed in a shimmering purple suit, entered the stage to greet the audience. She moved slightly differently from the human artists. Although she hid her aura, a faint supernatural energy surrounded her.

The other six circus shows she'd seen in the past weeks paled in comparison to this breathtaking spectacle. Artists did acrobatics on a trapeze, used aerial straps and silk, or balanced with stacked chairs. They were doing hand-to-hand acrobatics, trampolining, dancing, fire eating, and juggling. The acts themselves were ordinary, but the artists' distinguished movements stood out. A mixture of dancing, music, and clown silliness completed the experience.

Even though she followed the crowd outside after the performance, she didn't leave the premises. Instead, she sneaked along the giant tent and the trailers to find a place to confront the vampire privately.

A big trailer with blinds in front of the windows stood separate from the others. It offered the privacy a vampire required, so she climbed onto its roof and lay down to wait for the director's return. The venue still crawled with circus workers and artists running around, chatting with each other, and cleaning up.

Nights were cold at the end of November, but she wrapped up in the new winter coat she'd bought in Bratislava a week ago. After three hours, most of the circus workers had returned to their trailers, but the director wasn't among them.

Two hours later, the vampire returned from her nightly outing, still in her fancy stage outfit. Her shoulder-length, black hair framed her round face. She paused several meters from the trailer and looked straight at Lilah. "Is there a reason you're lying on my trailer?"

Heat rose to her face. Hiding on top of the vampire's trailer like a criminal didn't leave the best first impression. The idea of assaulting or robbing a vampire sounded ridiculous, but the vampire didn't know she knew her true nature. She jumped from the trailer and took a bow. "Sorry. I know this must look suspicious, but my intentions are good."

"What do you want from me?"

"You're Lexi, aren't you?" Considering the talent of her circus members, the vampire would be a wonderful teacher either way.

"I haven't used that name in a long time." Lexi furrowed her brows.

"A mutual acquaintance told me about you—the leader of a talented circus group, encouraging humans to perfect their movements beyond human boundaries. I need your help."

"With what? Do you wish to join a circus?"

"Not exactly." She let the hold on her powers slip for an instant to demonstrate she was more than a mere human, too. When Lexi's eyes widened, she suppressed her supernatural energy again. "I want to become stronger...strong enough to defeat a powerful vampire in a duel. Therefore, I've already asked others to train me.

"Skilled vampires taught me different fighting styles, and by drinking their blood, my body has surpassed human boundaries. There are still areas in which I'm lacking, though. I don't move as fast, smooth, or controlled as a vampire yet, so I hope you can help me with that."

"Although I've seen many oddities in the circus life, I have to admit you're quite something. I'm intrigued. However, if you want my assistance, you must prove yourself first."

"I'll do anything."

Lexi smiled. "Good. I like your attitude. Help at the circus, there's always plenty to do, and train with our artists. You'll learn most of the basics from them, better than I could teach you. If you're a good study, you can prove yourself by joining the performances. Only then will I step in and help you reach an even higher level of skill."

"All right." Being taught by humans sounded like a step backward, but these artists were extremely skilled. "Will you also give me some of your blood?"

"My blood?" Lexi frowned. "Well…I don't mind. I've never seen a human feed on vampires, but I guess there's a first for everything. And I want to see what you can do. What's your name?"

"I'm Lilah. What do you go by these days?"

"Lexi is fine in private—it *is* my name. Currently, I'm going by Sophie. Anyway, I'm tired. Circus life forces me to be awake during most of the day. You better get some sleep as well. Where are you staying?"

"Nowhere yet. Are there any hostels nearby?"

"I'm not sure…" She tilted her head, studying Lilah. "If you don't have anywhere else to go, you can stay in my trailer. I've got a spare bed."

"Sounds perfect, thank you! Don't you mind sharing your trailer with a stranger like me?"

"I offered, didn't I? With all the people I meet in my line of work, I'm an excellent judge of character. And you already know I'm a vampire, so there's nothing for me to worry about."

****

A soft jolt on her shoulder woke Lilah, and she opened her eyes to find Lexi in front of her. In contrast to the previous night, the vampire wore khaki pants and a plain white blouse.

"Get up. It's already ten," Lexi said.

Lilah blinked. Rays of light peeked through the blinds. "Ten? Why is it still light out?"

"It's ten a.m."

"What? Why are you waking me so early in the day?" she grumbled. "I usually sleep until late afternoon."

Lexi laughed. "You complain about getting up early to *me*? I'm the vampire. Get dressed, then I'll introduce you to the team."

Twenty minutes later, they were standing in the middle of the circus tent. Over forty artists and crew members huddled in small groups in the stands. They were chatting, eating breakfast, and planning tasks for the day.

"Morning, everyone." Although Lexi didn't raise her voice, the chatter quieted down and every face turned to her. "Let me introduce Lilah to you. She'll stay with us for a while and help around the circus. In return, I want each of our performers to teach her the basics of their art. Let her join your training sessions, challenge her, and maybe include her in your stage performance if she does well. Questions?"

"Does she have any experience performing?" a bulky guy with a Spanish accent asked.

"Not yet, but I'm a quick study," Lilah answered. "Please, give me a chance."

The circus members whispered among themselves. She caught pieces of their conversations—most of them complained about babysitting an inexperienced newbie.

"You must earn their respect," Lexi told her. "If they see you working hard, they'll warm up to you. Be patient and do your best."

Chapter 26

Lilah helped with show preparations, carried heavy equipment on her own, and sold tickets at the entrance. Despite her efforts, the circus workers kept their distance and only spoke with her when necessary. If it wasn't for Lexi, who used every chance to chat with her, she would have left after a few days. Since she'd barely met any female vampires during her journey, hearing about Lexi's life and experiences fascinated her.

On her fifth day, she was cleaning up after the evening performance when Lexi checked on her.

"Why are female vampires so rare? Or are they merely better at hiding in plain sight?" she asked.

Lexi stiffened. "No, we are rare."

"Why?"

"Most women won't last long in this brutal world dominated by blood and power," Lexi said with a pained expression. "Like male humans, male vampires often consider females as weak and treat them accordingly. Their intentions aren't always bad. Some think they're doing us a favor by patronizing us because they believe we can't take care of ourselves. Most women can't stand the oppression. The life of those who've stood their ground is a constant struggle. Centuries-old prejudices rule our society, and many men consider women too fragile and not worthy of becoming vampires."

"How have you dealt with these obstacles?"

"I separated from my sire and any men who thought they knew what's best for me early on. Since I've lived the circus life for as long as I can remember, I always had to prove myself and had something to live for. I doubt I'd have come this far if I'd been born a simple peasant girl." Lilah gulped, but Lexi smiled at her. "Us women must stick together and show everyone what we're made of. I like women going their own way and surpassing the limits society put on us, which is also the reason I agreed to help you."

She returned the smile. "Limits exist to be broken."

****

The next morning, a petite woman with shoulder-length, golden hair and blue eyes, younger than Lilah, approached her during breakfast.

"Hey there, I'm Vanessa."

"Hello, Vanessa." Lilah licked some leftover jam off her lips. "What can I do for you?"

Vanessa smiled shyly. "Sophie said we're supposed to teach you. I think a training partner sounds fun, so…you can join me today."

"I'd love to! What's your act?"

"My specialty is aerial silk. Follow me to the training hall once you're ready."

****

Her mouth went dry when Vanessa demonstrated her enthralling moves. With the help of the fabric, she almost appeared to fly. She wrapped herself in the silk, struck different poses, and let her body drop several meters before climbing back up. Her earlier shyness evaporated during her act.

"It's not as hard as it looks." Vanessa smiled encouragingly. "From what I can tell, you're already pretty good at controlling your body. You just need to get used to working with the fabric."

They started with simple movements on the ground. Soon, Lilah pulled herself up into the air with the soft silk rope. After a few days, she moved comfortably with and around the fabric high above the ground.

Consuming Lexi's strengthening vampire blood soothed her nerves. Apart from protecting her body, it also helped her progress quickly, which impressed Vanessa.

"I don't know how you do it, but I've spent years on learning all the skills you learned in two weeks."

"It's all thanks to your guidance." She avoided Vanessa's gaze. She couldn't tell her why she learned so fast.

"I doubt it..." Vanessa chuckled. "But I think it's cool. How about joining me for my performance tonight?"

She felt the blood leave her face. "Performance? I don't think I...I mean, I feel flattered, but I'm still a beginner."

"You'll be fine."

Her chest tightened at the prospect of performing in front of an audience, but she didn't want to disappoint Lexi or Vanessa. At least no one in Hungary would recognize her. And yet her heart beat like a drum before their performance.

She pinned her long hair up and put on makeup. Dressing up made everything seem unreal. Their stage outfits looked almost like bathing suits, except they glittered in the artificial light. The two women entered the stage side by side, headed straight to the aerial silk ropes in the center, and climbed up.

Just like during their training, she mirrored Vanessa's every move. Focusing solely on her and her partner's movements entranced her. She didn't even notice the audience until they started clapping at the end of the act. Only then did the thrill of the situation hit her, and she felt light-headed.

"Well-done," Lexi greeted them afterward. "Lilah, I believe you're ready to move on to the next skill."

"Already?" Vanessa pouted.

"I'm sure I'll still find time to train with you or join you onstage sometimes." She smiled. "Learning a new skill sounds fun, though."

As she had proven her ability to perform, finding someone to train her was easier than before. After the aerial silk, she learned hand-to-hand techniques with a group of three Spanish acrobats. Then she did trampolining, followed by balancing and trapeze acrobatics. She spent one or two weeks on an act before proving her skill onstage each time.

After five different performances, Lexi agreed to give her private training lessons. She still assisted with circus preparations and often joined the evening shows, though. After getting over her first stage fright, she loved the thrill of performing.

****

"What did the vampire you're trying to kill ever do to you?" Lexi asked Lilah one day after their training session.

Kill? I don't intend to kill anyone. Who is she—Oh! "You've misunderstood. I don't plan to kill him. I merely wish to defeat him in battle."

"Why?" Lexi tilted her head.

"It's hard to explain...Call it love...or

stubbornness." She smiled shyly.

"You're speaking in riddles, girl. If you love this vampire, why do you intend to fight him?"

"To coerce him into overcoming his stupid, entrenched ways of thinking." She sighed. She hadn't talked about Cain in a long time.

"Come on, give me more than that. We're friends, aren't we?"

A fond smile formed on her lips. They'd shared many late-night chats and laughs in the past months. Lexi *had* become a close friend. She hoped her friend wouldn't judge her.

"As you know, I've lived and trained with different vampires for over two and a half years now…"

"Was your beloved one of them?"

She nodded. "I spent the first year with him and fell in love. But he refused my plea for him to turn me, saying he'd never create a vampire, because of his beliefs. When I kept prodding, he made an unfair proposal. If I won in a battle against him, he'd fulfill my wish. If I lost, he'd kill me."

She ignored Lexi's shocked gasp and continued with a sigh. "I suppose he simply meant to deter me…to protect me in his own way. Still, I'd pushed him too far, and he abandoned me. And yet, I love him. By defeating him in a fight and forcing him to turn me, I'll make him realize how wrong his beliefs are."

"What if you can't change his mind?"

"I'm an optimist—I have to be. So I believe we can work it out and become happy together."

Lexi watched her with sympathetic eyes. "He doesn't sound like he's worth it. Never sacrifice your life for a man."

"I won't," she said decidedly. "Even without him, I aspire to become a vampire. The moment I set my eyes on this world, I knew I belonged here. I've never felt so alive."

"I'm glad. Men rarely see a woman's potential, so promise me you'll never let them hold you back. Never let them destroy your dreams."

"I promise."

Lexi's face softened as she studied Lilah. "If you can't convince him, or if you change your mind and quit running after him, you have another option. Stay here with us. I'd be happy to turn you."

Lilah's eyes widened.

"Believe me, I don't make such an offer lightly. There will always be a deep connection between a vampire and their sire, so I understand if you prefer to forge this bond with him. Siring a strong-willed person like you would still be an honor for me."

"Thank you," she said, and her eyes glistened. "I'm touched, and your offer honors me, but I can't accept it. I long for *him* to turn me. My wish has kept me going for so long, and it's already brought me this far, so I can't take an easy way out."

"I understand, and I'd expect nothing less from you. However, my offer will still stand if you change your mind one day."

She hugged her friend to hide the tears building in her eyes.

Chapter 27

Lilah took a final bow as the audience applauded her performance for the last time. After five wonderful months at the circus, she had to leave if she wanted to get closer to her goal.

"Great job again!" Vanessa's eyes glowed as she met her backstage. "Thanks for joining me."

"No, thank you for everything you taught me." A lump built in her throat.

"How about we change into something more comfy and then meet for a beer in my trailer?"

"Sure."

Fifty minutes later, she knocked on her friend's trailer. Vanessa opened the door with an apologetic smile. "Hey, Lilah. Apparently, I've lost my hairpin backstage. Will you help me search?"

"Um, okay."

When they entered the tent through a rear entrance, darkness enveloped them. She felt around for a switch and turned on the light.

A roar came from the stage. "Surprise!"

Lexi and the other circus members gathered around a makeshift table filled with multicultural snacks, beer, a bowl of punch, and other treats.

"We couldn't let you leave without a goodbye party." Vanessa grinned. "Everyone brought their favorite food or booze."

How could she say goodbye when they showered her with kindness and love? They were like family. She sobbed. "Wow, I don't know what to say."

"I do," Lexi said. "When you came to us, you told me you'd only stay for a while. Yet, we've grown fond of you. With your enthusiasm, your talent, and your endurance, it's hard to believe you haven't lived the circus life before. You've become part of our family, and I think I speak for everyone when I say we'll miss you. I know the world is calling, and I understand your reasons for leaving. Don't forget, you'll always have a place with us, no matter what happens."

The others nodded in agreement.

"Thank you." She fought back her tears. "I'll never forget my time with you. Even though it passed quickly, I've learned a lot and made so many precious memories, thanks to all of you."

They celebrated until the first sunbeams crept into the tent, and she returned to her bed in Lexi's trailer for a nap. Before she fell asleep, Lexi asked her where she planned to go next.

"I don't think I'm ready to face *him* yet," she replied. "By now, I've worked on my stealth, my strength, my weapon skills, and my movements. The bottom line is, I've enhanced skills most humans can learn, which is not enough. From what I've heard, some vampires possess psychic abilities. If I learned such skills and knew how to counter them, I'd be virtually invincible. Do you know anyone with outstanding telepathic abilities?"

"Not personally. I've heard rumors of a vampire with almost magical powers, living somewhere near Salzburg."

"It's worth a try," she mumbled before falling asleep.

When she woke around noon, everyone was busy preparing for the afternoon performance. She left without another goodbye since she didn't want to disturb them, and part of her feared changing her resolve to leave if she faced them again. After walking to the station, she took an express train to Salzburg and slept most of the journey.

****

Lilah went for a walk to get to know the area on this nice spring evening. Wandering through the narrow streets and beautiful gardens of the old city for hours didn't amount to much. After dusk, she strolled up to the Hohensalzburg fortress, as it offered a magnificent view. It was closed at night, but she didn't care. She climbed up the castle walls to observe the sleeping city. Everything was quiet, and there were no signs of vampires. Around dawn, she rented a bed in a hostel to catch some sleep before resuming her search.

How should she find a vampire without knowing if he even existed? After three days with no vampire sightings, she researched the history of Salzburg to look for clues. Rummaging through books at the local library revealed the city's dark past of witch trials. Were witches real? She didn't know the answer, but who was she to doubt their existence? Besides, chances were people mistook a vampire with psychic abilities for a witch.

With newfound hope, she spent every night out on the streets, searching. After two weeks, she noticed a supernatural aura on the outskirts of Salzburg. Shortly after arriving in the area, she spotted a male vampire with blond, curly hair, feeding on a girl in an alley. When he let the girl drop to the ground, she hid around a street corner and held her breath to hide her presence. She planned to get a rough estimate of his powers before revealing herself to him.

The vampire didn't leave right away. Had he noticed her, or what was he waiting for?

Finally, she felt his aura move in the opposite direction. She let go of her breath and followed him at a distance. When she passed the girl on the ground, she bent down to check her pulse. The girl breathed evenly, as if she were dreaming. She kept following the vampire, but after taking several turns, she lost track of him.

"Damn it," she whispered. He'd either teleported, taken an unexpected turn, or entered one of the many houses in the area. Since she couldn't feel his energy anymore, the teleportation theory was the most probable one. Why did he walk these streets in the first place if he knew how to teleport? Something didn't add up.

Using a fire escape on the side of an older apartment house, she climbed on top of the two-story building to get a better view of her surroundings. She let her eyes wander. When she saw the building on the opposite side of the alley, she froze. The vampire stood on its roof, watching her.

Thanks to the moonlight, she saw him clearly. With a green hoodie, a pair of jeans, and sneakers, he appeared youthful. She didn't let appearances fool her, though. Considering he'd noticed her and cloaked his presence, she didn't underestimate him.

He spoke first. "You're either very brave, very stupid, or both."

"Well, out of these options, I hope only the first one applies. I don't want any trouble. I'm looking for help."

To emphasize her intentions, she went down on one knee, bowing her head to show respect.

"Do you expect me to believe you, hunter girl?"

She sighed. Why did every vampire mistake her for a hunter?

"I'm not a hunter, although I know how to defend myself." Lilah pulled her retractable staff out of a pouch attached to her belt. She got up and extended it to its full length. "I'm also more than willing to give you a taste of my powers."

"Do you think I'm dumb enough to let you raise your weapon against me?"

"If you don't wish to fight, how about you listen to what I have to say? I'm sure we can figure something out."

He shook his head. "I don't like either option, so I'll choose option number three and kill you."

The vampire clicked his tongue three times. Then he stormed toward her, crossing the abyss between the two buildings in a second. She had planned to defend herself by spinning her staff, but she could not move. Her body did not react. Somehow, he'd frozen her.

The vampire stopped less than a meter from her and smirked. "Didn't you just give me a speech about showing me your power? Well? Come at me, will you?"

She tried again, but nothing happened. She couldn't move a muscle. A shudder went through her as he pushed her hair to the side and leaned in close, sniffing her neck.

"Let's not drag the inevitable out any longer. I'll end your pathetic performance," he whispered into her ear.

A tear ran down her face. Would she die now? Had her training been for nothing? How did he render her powerless, with no effort?

Elli Morgan

She gasped when his fangs broke her skin. In this painful moment, she briefly regained control of her body. But it was too late, and everything went black.

Chapter 28

Lilah awoke on the floor of a dark cellar, naked except for her panties and sports bra, with chains around her wrists and her neck. A vague sense of déjà vu hit her, and her chest constricted. Unlike the last time she'd found herself in such a dire situation, no one was coming to her rescue. On the plus side, the room wasn't pitch-black. A faint light from a small window on the opposite wall penetrated the darkness. And despite the chains, she could still move within a radius of about two meters.

Somehow, she had to rescue herself. A harsh pull on the chains didn't amount to anything. The material was quite durable. As the shackles around her wrists hung rather loosely, she considered slipping out of them by dislocating her thumb bones. The chain around her neck would keep her from escaping, though, which was reason enough to dismiss the painful idea.

Since the vampire had stripped her, she didn't have access to her weapons. Could she wrestle him down? With his power of freezing her movements combined with being chained to the wall, she didn't stand a chance. What had he planned? And why hadn't he killed her? She was glad to be alive. But how long would the sentiment last if he was anything like Lucious?

She was still pondering her options when the vampire entered the room. Adrenaline shot through her body, and she let her instincts take over. With a hiss, she went down on all fours, ready to jump at him or move out of his reach if he came too close.

He watched her with an amused expression. "What do you think you're doing?"

She glowered at him.

When he took a few steps toward her, she moved to the far corner of the room, crouched down, and hugged her arms around her legs.

"You remind me of a scared kitten." He chuckled.

"Well, what would you do in my place? Give up and accept my fate?" she growled.

"What fate? I haven't decided what I'm going to do with you yet. Stop fooling around and talk to me properly."

She swallowed. A chance to talk was the best she'd get in this situation, so she calmed herself with deep breaths, kneeled, and bowed her head.

"Much better," the vampire said. "Now, let's start again. I'm Daniel. What's your name?"

"Lilah."

"All right, Lilah. Tell me, why did you follow me last night?"

"I've heard rumors about a vampire with powerful psychic abilities living in Salzburg. When I sensed your supernatural energy, I hoped you were the one. I followed you to learn more about you first."

"First?" Daniel interrupted her. "What were you planning to do after gathering information? Were you planning to hunt me down?"

"No." She shook her head. "I'm looking for a mentor to help me become stronger."

"Why?"

"Because there's a powerful vampire I must defeat.

Thanks to other vampires who assisted me, I've come close to my goal. Although I am stronger than a lot of vampires, I'm still human. And I'm vulnerable to a vampire's psychic abilities, as last night has proven without doubt. So I yearn to learn how to overcome telepathic assaults and how to use simple psychic tricks myself. After what I saw last night, I'd like you to teach me those skills, but I know I'm in no position to ask for anything right now."

"You're right, it's not your place to ask for anything, human." He approached her and placed his hand on her chin to lift her head, forcing her to meet his iridescent green eyes. "And if I didn't know you were telling the truth, I'd rip out your tongue for talking bullshit."

"How do you know I'm not lying?" she stammered.

"I can read your mind, and I saw flashes of your memories while drinking your blood. They aroused my interest enough to keep you alive. It's also the answer to your unspoken question why I haven't killed you yet."

Her face flushed. What had Daniel seen in her memories? She couldn't protect the identities of the vampires who'd helped her against such an ability.

"I'm not interested in other vampires' secrets and schemes. You interest me, though," he commented on her thought.

"What do you plan to do with me?" The question was nothing more than a whisper.

He shrugged and turned to leave. "I'll think about it."

Would he leave her with trembling uncertainty? She needed to gauge his intentions. "If you're leaving me here, at least give me some clothes and water."

He studied her with a gleam in his eyes. "You're not

shy at all, are you?"

"If you're reading my thoughts, I may as well say what I'm thinking, right?" She gulped.

He laughed. Her body trembled as he left and closed the door behind him.

I'll die here miserably, won't I?

He returned a few minutes later with a pile of clothes, a blanket, a bottle of water, and a pillow.

Maybe I won't.

"Get up." He handed her a pair of pants. They were hers, but he'd removed the belt. She stood on wobbly legs as she put them on.

Daniel laid the remaining clothes on the floor. "I'll remove the chains for a moment so you can get dressed. Once you're done, I'll put them back on. You won't try to run, and you won't resist. Do you understand?"

She nodded. If he offered her a chance to prove her intentions, she wouldn't blow it. Besides, she couldn't fight his psychic powers.

He released her, and she put on her T-shirt and sweater with deliberately slow movements. Then she held up her hands for him to chain her up again.

"Thank you," she said. "Why'd you undress me, anyway?"

He shrugged. "To make sure you had no weapons hidden on your body."

After he'd left her on her own, her knees buckled, and she sank to the floor. He didn't behave cruelly. He was simply...cautious? She drank a mouthful of water and tried to make herself comfortable, but the pillow and blanket didn't help much. As her situation could be so much worse, she accepted it without complaint.

A few hours later, the door opened with a squeak

and woke her from a restless sleep. Daniel brought her a paper bag filled with food. Her mouth watered when the smell of a burger with fries hit her nose.

"Thanks." She accepted the food and dug right in.

****

When Daniel returned the next evening, she felt queasy. Had he decided her fate? She kneeled down in anticipation.

"To sum up, you've asked me to teach you how to withstand or counter my powers, which doesn't put me in a favorable position, now, does it?"

"If you put it that way, you make it sound like a bad idea," she replied with a quiver in her voice.

"At least, I don't see what's in it for me. Why should I train you and risk grooming a formidable foe?"

"I have no intention of becoming your foe. My only goal is to become stronger," she argued. "I usually offer my blood to the vampires helping me. Considering my current position, I guess the offer doesn't seem very compelling to you."

"Not really," he agreed.

Her eyes found his. "Look at me. I can't offer you anything except for my blood, my companionship, and my loyalty. If it's not enough, I can't do anything to change your mind."

She took an audible breath. "I know the risks of living in this world. Every time I go out and confront a vampire, I might end up dead. I accepted this reality a long time ago, and I'm prepared to look fate in the eye."

"I expected you to make a more compelling case for your life."

You and me both, but I've fooled myself long enough. "I'm under no illusions. I know my fate lies in your hands, and there's nothing I can do if you wish to kill me. So I won't bore you with pleading for my life."

"Are you so eager to die?" He squatted down to her level.

"No, I love my life. But the excitement and danger I face every day are an essential part of what I love about it. They make me feel alive."

"You make taking risks sound like something worth doing."

"It *can* be." She smiled. She needed him to take a risk on her. Most vampires loved taking risks to break the routine of their long lives.

He chuckled. "Let's say I'm giving you a chance. How would me helping you play out?"

"However you want it to. The vampires who've helped me so far offered me accommodations in their homes. They spent several hours training me every day, fed me their blood, and sometimes fed on me. Vampire blood allows my body to surpass human limits. With your potentially powerful blood, I might even develop psychic abilities."

He pondered her request for a few minutes, which felt like an eternity. Finally, he smiled. "You've piqued my curiosity."

Chapter 29

Daniel lived in a small town house outside the city. The ground floor comprised a living room with a built-in kitchen, while the upper floor offered two bedrooms and a bathroom. The only unusual thing about his house was the cellar equipped with chains. Factoring in his relaxed and youthful appearance, he did a good job of blending into the human world.

"It's easier to hide in plain sight," he commented on Lilah's thoughts. "I don't want any trouble, which is why I keep to myself."

She bit her lip, trying not to let her irritation at him reading her mind show. "Isn't it boring?" she asked.

"Sometimes, but it's safe."

"You always put your safety above everything, don't you?"

He shrugged. "What's wrong with playing it safe? I've been alive long enough to know what cruelties humans and vampires are capable of."

"So letting people in is a risk? Maybe you're right, but don't you think it's much riskier to shut everyone out and end up all alone? You might live an eternal life if you avoid risks, but is it worth living?"

"I don't mind living this way," he said. "And you're still alive, so I'm taking a risk right now."

"A calculated one, considering you can read my thoughts and intentions."

"Whatever. Don't make me change my mind and put you back in chains," he threatened with a grin.

"So…I guess I'm not getting my weapons back?"

"Who can read thoughts now?"

She groaned, but she didn't really mind. She appreciated him letting her roam his house freely, which was a major improvement compared to him locking her in the cellar. Besides, she had not sought him out to work on her weapon skills. "How can I learn psychic abilities?"

"What do you know about psychology?"

"Not much."

"Then I propose you start by reading into the subject to gain a basic understanding of its concepts." He showed her a large shelf in his living room, filled with hundreds of textbooks. "I've got quite a collection now. These books helped me develop my skills."

She gaped. "Even though I like reading, it'll take months or even years to read them all."

"You don't have to." He chose a book on human behavior, another one on persuasion, and a third on hypnosis. "These should give you an extensive introduction into the topics. Once you're done with them, we can discuss the content and how the knowledge helps you."

"Okay." She frowned. This was definitely a novel way of training.

With the first book in hand, she planted herself in an armchair. Daniel also picked a book and stretched out on the living room couch, from where he kept an eye on her.

****

"How about giving me some blood?" Lilah asked at the end of her third night of reading.

Daniel looked up from his book. "Blood for blood?"

"Fine with me." She wasn't squeamish about letting him drink from her veins—he'd already had plenty of opportunities to kill her.

He sat up and motioned for her to come over. She plopped down onto the couch next to him and bared her throat. He pulled her close, so she was almost on his lap.

A gasp escaped her lips as he bit her. She expected a short sting of pain. She didn't expect the assault of pleasure which followed. Heat and a tingling she hadn't felt since Cain abandoned her flooded her senses. Why did Daniel make her feel this way? Most vampires only numbed the pain. She sagged onto his lap once he released her. His naughty grin dared her to protest, but she only averted her gaze. *It's not like I can complain about it feeling too good.* Was it wrong to revel in the ecstasy of his weirdly intimate bite? Would Cain mind if he knew? She squashed the thought. Cain wasn't there, and he surely didn't fast just because she wasn't by his side.

"My turn now," she said.

****

Once Lilah finished reading the books, they talked about the concepts of his psychic abilities and how to achieve similar effects with no special powers. A lot of it came down to simple psychological tricks.

At first, Daniel was reluctant to explain how to counter psychic attacks, but after a while, he got over his hesitation and enjoyed testing different strategies with her. They also tackled countering his ability to freeze her movements.

"How does it work?" she asked seconds before he froze her again by making three weird sounds with his tongue.

"It's hypnosis," he explained. "With these sounds, I get you to focus on my face. As soon as your eyes lock with mine, I send your body a subconscious command and put you into a trance. You won't freeze if you avoid my gaze."

Your advice is a little too late since you've already frozen me, she thought, annoyed, as she could not speak.

He chuckled. "Yes, it is. Do you remember how you broke out of my hypnosis before?"

His statement confused her. He'd only frozen her once, on the night they'd met. He'd fed on her while letting her believe she'd die. She couldn't fight him off, but she remembered regaining control of her body right before falling unconscious. *How?*

"Pain's the answer," he suggested.

Of course. Back then, the trance broke when his fangs had pierced her skin. Waiting for her enemy to hurt her didn't seem like a practical solution in a serious fight, though.

He waited a bit before he elaborated. "You merely believe you can't move, but it's all in your head. There's nothing keeping you frozen. If you concentrate hard, you should be able to move at least a little. Try to pinch yourself or bite your tongue or something."

She struggled for a while, with no success.

"If you can't free yourself, I'll break the trance by biting you." He grinned.

As he'd feed on her either way, the threat didn't faze her. It also didn't encourage her enough to overcome the hypnosis. After watching her for fifteen minutes, he made good on his words. His bite only hurt for a second before he turned it into a pleasurable experience. The sensations left her weak in the knees.

She panted. "Are you sure it's possible to move while being in your trance?"

"Not really. But considering your abilities, I didn't put it past you to get it done on your first try."

"Well, sorry to disappoint," she said grumpily.

"We have to work on your willpower. Let's try a meditation technique."

They kept practicing, and after several meditation exercises and countless tries, she eventually bit into her cheek, freeing herself.

Apart from breaking free of psychic abilities, she learned useful tricks aimed at anticipating her opponent's movements and intentions by paying attention to certain cues. Daniel also taught her how to hide her thoughts from vampires like him.

During their time together, she gradually learned more about his past. Ignorant people had accused him of witchcraft back in 1680. They based their claims on his vast knowledge and his ability to predict human behavior because of his observant nature and his interest in psychology. At the same time, his talents caught the attention of a vampire, who turned him before his execution.

Yet, the prejudice and cruelty of people had scarred him, and he withdrew from social life. With his predisposition and his continued interest in psychology, he developed genuine psychic abilities as his vampiric powers grew.

****

After six months with Daniel, a restlessness overcame her.

He noticed her eagerness to move on. "Do you

believe you're ready to face your last opponent?"

"I'll never know until I try."

"True, but since your life's on the line, shouldn't you be more careful?"

"You know I like taking risks. Besides, I don't think I can enhance my powers much more. I'll waste time if I keep training and postpone facing him."

"What if the time you waste is the only time left?" His eyes locked with hers, pleading with her to reconsider.

"I'd rather die for my dream than waste my life away."

"I figured as much…Although I'll be sad to see you go, I won't stop you," he conceded. "I'd invite you to stay with me forever if I didn't know you'd reject me because there's already someone else in your heart."

He shook his head, as if to clear the thought from his mind. "It's okay, though. I can feel your determination, and I wish you the best."

She sucked in a breath. She hadn't expected his honest confession and how much he cared for her. "Thank you…I appreciate your honesty and everything you've done for me."

"Where will you go? Do you know where to find him?"

"No." She shook her head. "I never knew the exact location of his home, but I figured I could wait for him at the royal castle. If I wait long enough, he's bound to come by sometime."

He stared at her with wide eyes.

"At least it's a plan." She grinned at him. "Care to drop me off?"

Chapter 30

After Daniel had failed to talk Lilah out of her plan,
he returned her weapons and dropped her off about four
kilometers from the royal castle.

"It's as far as I can take you since I don't want to run
into other vampires. You'll be on your own from now
on, so I hope you know what you're doing." He shot her
a worried glance.

"I'll be fine." She smiled at him. "Thank you for
everything."

"Goodbye." He vanished with a forced smile.

She followed the only route leading to the castle
until she spotted the majestic building in the distance.
The sun rising from behind the mountain offered a
magical sight. As she didn't want anyone to notice her
approach, she left the road and wandered through the
surrounding woods. She also suppressed her thoughts
and her aura to stay unnoticed.

The terrain was uneven and overgrown, and the
vegetation hid her from sight. The rays of the sun
shimmered through the forest and helped her find her
way. They also kept the number of vampires in the area
to a minimum.

After a three-hour hike, she arrived at an outer wall
at the back of the castle grounds. She climbed up a
nearby tree, jumped onto the wall, and then down into
the inner yard. Finding a way into the castle was no

challenge, either. She sneaked through an open window and found herself in a storage room filled with food, alcohol, and an oversized fridge with perishables. Even though vampires didn't eat, their human pets needed nourishment. Her mouth watered at the sight of a red apple, so she ate it.

She planned to hide close to the throne hall, where she hoped to eavesdrop on the matters at court and to pick up news regarding Cain's whereabouts. With her destination in mind, she moved as quietly as possible through empty hallways.

She arrived at the main entrance, where a lone guard leaned against the wall next to the door. Even from afar, she heard him snore. Taking advantage of his carelessness, she tiptoed to the door, opened it a crack, and peered inside.

Since it was empty, she slipped into the hall and closed the door behind her. An area closed off with tarpaulin offered a perfect hiding space with front-row seats to the court. The tarpaulin concealed a broken statue while leaving enough space for her to make herself comfortable. Eventually, she dozed off while waiting for something to happen.

She woke up to the familiar voice of the king. "…any news from London?"

"Yes, but it's not good. The vampires in question have become even more brazen. They're not only living among humans without hiding their differences, they also display their speed, strength, and hunger for blood. It'll be a matter of time until the first human suspects it's more than a special effect," an unknown voice reported.

"Send someone there to make them realize the seriousness of their transgressions."

Uh-oh. Are they talking about Kevin and his punk-band sire?

"Yes, Your Majesty."

They discussed a group of hunters causing trouble in Oslo next, but she ceased listening. Nothing caught her attention until the king sent everyone out without a reason.

As soon as his servants had closed the doors, his voice echoed through the hall. "Did you think you could hide from me in *my* castle, human?"

How had he noticed her? Sighing in defeat, she came out from behind the tarpaulin, walked to the throne, and kneeled down a few meters from him.

The king eyed her. "You're the human who used to be Cain's pet."

"Yes, Your Majesty," she said. *No need to get hung up on the term "pet."*

"What are you doing here?"

"I'm looking for Cain or clues to his whereabouts."

"Why? What happened after your visit to court?"

"I asked Cain to turn me into a vampire, and he abandoned me. More precisely, he gave me an ultimatum I could not accept. He told me to fight him. If I won, he'd fulfill my wish, otherwise he'd kill me. Back then, I didn't stand a chance against him." She grimaced. "But it's different now. After spending the last two years training with every powerful vampire I encountered, I'm ready to take him up on his challenge…I just need to find him first."

He chuckled. "I knew you'd make an interesting vampire. You're already quite impressive for a human. I can feel the power in you. Will you let me drink your blood to get a taste of the things you've experienced in our world?"

She hesitated. The circumstances differed from the last time he'd seen her memories through her blood, since she hadn't yet met the vampires whose identities she promised to keep safe. Letting their king find out about them wasn't an option.

"I don't mind offering my blood, Your Majesty. Nevertheless, I've only come this far thanks to several vampires, and I don't want to reveal anything about them against their wishes."

He smiled. "I appreciate loyalty. However, I'm more interested in your experiences than in some vampire's secrets. Do you know you can control the images I receive through your blood? Why don't you decide what I may see? I'll make it worth your while."

"I can't refuse a king's request, now, can I?" She approached the throne, kneeled, and offered her wrist.

"Think of what you want to show me," he instructed her before biting into her flesh.

She thought about leaving her old home, traveling through Europe on her search for vampires, battling at the fight club, training on a Greek island, performing at the circus, and meditating to strengthen her willpower. She deliberately left out any memories regarding Lucious. His father would recognize him at once.

"You've come a long way," the king said after closing his bite marks. "I hope you'll achieve your goal. You'd complement Cain perfectly."

"What do you mean?"

"Cain's a loner. Until he met you, he never cared for anything. And yet, he's knowledgeable and an experienced fighter. If he tried, he could make it far in our world. You are young, impulsive, and human. Yet, you strive for something more. You fight hard to get what you desire, and you find your allies along the way. With the two of you together, there is nothing you can't achieve."

"I hope I can live up to your expectations, Your Majesty," she mumbled while a flush of heat crept across her cheeks from the unexpected praise.

"I hope so, too. In fact, I want to support you." He bit into his wrist.

She eagerly accepted the blood he offered.

"Not even a handful of beings have fed on my blood. Royal blood is powerful, so make the most of it," he said once she'd finished drinking.

"I'm well aware of the power. Thank you, Your Majesty, for your faith in me."

"I'll also reunite you with Cain. You can stay here while I send for him. He should arrive within a week."

Part III

HOME

The end of the road
when the moon comes full circle—
a moment of truth.

Chapter 31

To avoid attracting the attention of other vampires at the castle, Lilah hid her aura and stayed in the king's royal chambers behind the door at the end of the throne hall. They comprised four fancy bedrooms, a huge lounge area, and a bathroom with a whirlpool.

Most of the furniture was antique, and several statues and paintings of historical events decorated the rooms. She felt insecure about sharing living quarters with the vampire king, but she saw little of him because he tended to his business most of the time. He still fed her some of his blood every night.

On her fourth night there, she was doing push-ups as part of a daily exercise program when a familiar aura approached the castle. *Cain.* Her heart bounced in her chest, and she rushed to the door of the throne hall. Part of her yearned to run straight into his arms, and another part was terrified of facing him after all this time.

Her entire future, everything she'd worked for, depended on what happened next. The thought paralyzed her, which was a good thing because the king had ordered her to stay in his chambers until he called for her.

Through the door, she heard a guard announce Cain's presence.

"Thank you. Everyone else, please leave," the king said.

Feet shuffled on the floor, and a heavy door closed

with a thump.

"I'm here as requested, Your Majesty. Why did you call for me?"

Her knees buckled at the sound of Cain's voice.

"Thank you for coming. I didn't call you here for my sake, though," the king said. "Considering she's waiting anxiously behind the door, maybe we should invite her to join us?"

"Who's waiting behind the door?" Cain asked.

"Come in, Lilah," the king said.

Her hand shook as she reached for the door handle. She entered the hall with weak knees, and when her gaze landed on Cain, shyness overcame her. Was he happy to see her? Did he still care for her at all, or had he moved on? Afraid to look him in the eye, she fixated on the floor as she walked toward him.

"What's the meaning of this?" he asked, not a hint of emotion in his voice.

Her eyes wandered to his face for a fraction of a second. His expression was a mixture of surprise, hurt, and fear. Yet he didn't meet her fleeting glance. His eyes fixated on the king.

"What do you mean?" the king returned the question.

She arrived at Cain's side and kneeled next to him, facing the king. Her heart raced, but their conversation gave her a chance to collect herself.

"What is she doing here? She's supposed to be back in her human world—safe," Cain rephrased his question.

His concern for her safety soothed her nerves, and she took a deep breath.

"I didn't bring her here," the king refuted the unspoken accusation. "She came on her own, and from what I can tell, she doesn't want to be a part of the safe world you picked for her. She's chosen her own path."

"It still doesn't explain what she's *doing* here," he said once again.

"The brief answer is, she's asked for my help to get in touch with you. You better ask *her* for the long one," the king replied patiently.

Cain still didn't address her. Instead, he kept focusing on the king. "Why are you helping her? What's your interest in this human, Your Majesty?"

"She's got potential. I wish to see where it'll lead her and how she'll affect you. But you better talk to her now. I'll give you two a moment alone." With these words, the king left the throne hall, entering the royal chambers.

She and Cain had no choice but to face each other. He got up, turned around, and finally looked at her. She forced herself to meet his gaze.

"I assumed you'd died," he said, his voice heavy with emotions.

"Why?" An icy shiver ran down her spine.

"Six months after leaving you, I came to check how you were doing. I didn't find a trace of you. Only your mother, mourning your loss."

"Oh shit." She sighed. Even though she had not died, her mum had lost her daughter. "Well…as you can see, I didn't die. I merely turned my back on my old life."

"Why?"

"After everything you've shown me, did you honestly expect me to return to the life I never wanted?"

"Yes. It's the life you were born into."

"You weren't born a vampire either, were you?" she countered. "It's my life. I decide how and where I want to live it. With everything I've experienced in the past two years, I'm convinced I've made the right decision."

"What have you been doing during these two years?"

Better not to reveal too much yet. "I've traveled through Europe, training. On my journey, I met all kinds of vampires, among them businessmen and artists. They've shown me what life can be like."

"And why are you seeking me out now?"

"Because I've missed you," she said, and his expression softened. Then she added, "And I haven't forgotten your offer. Back then, you didn't give me a chance to accept or decline. So I'll answer now. I'm ready to face you in a fight for my life."

"You're crazy." He turned away from her.

Before he withdrew any further, she stood up and grabbed his arm. "I'm not crazy. I know what I want and what it takes. You told me your price over two years ago. I'm willing to pay it now. You aren't going back on your word, are you?" Her voice was firm. There was no turning back.

He faced her, accusation and pain in his eyes. "I've already thought you'd died once before. Do you honestly believe I'd let you choose death now?"

"I've told you before I'm not choosing death. I'm choosing eternal life, preferably by your side, and I'll risk everything to get it. And don't tell me I don't know what I'm talking about. I've seen more than enough of your world. By now, it's also mine, and I ache to claim my place in it."

His gaze darted to the floor. "You're still human…You'll never beat me."

"You don't know how much I've grown. I accepted

the possibility of dying long ago. If you don't believe me, I'll fight you right here and now to show you my determination."

"Why can't you live your life and be content with what you've got?" His voice shook.

"Why should I accept the sky is the limit when there's an entire world beyond what most humans perceive? Life can offer so much more, and I want it all. Anything less won't satisfy me."

Cain shook his head in defeat. "It's impossible to talk sense into you, and you've even won the king over…You have my back against the wall. Forcing me to take your life is cruel, you know?"

"Don't turn this around on me. I'm not cruel. You're the one who's trying to keep me from what I crave."

The door to the king's chambers opened, and the king entered. She and Cain fell silent and kneeled.

The king positioned himself on his throne. "Even though it's entertaining to listen to your quarrel, you're in the throne hall, and I have other issues to attend to. I recommend taking your business elsewhere."

"I'm sorry," Cain said. "We'll leave right away."

He got to his feet, took a bow, and turned to leave.

"Oh, and Cain," the king added, "I'm looking forward to Lilah's introduction to court once you've turned her."

He didn't react to the king's suggestion.

"Thank you," she mouthed at the king. She got up, bowed to him, and followed Cain.

Chapter 32

After leaving the throne hall, Cain dashed through the corridors, exited the castle through the main gate, and continued down the road.

Lilah hurried after him. "Do you think you can run from me?"

"No."

"Then stop and talk to me!"

He jerked to a halt and turned to look at her. She sucked in a sharp breath at the sight of his pained expression.

"Not now." His voice pleaded with her.

She nodded slowly. "Okay."

His arms enclosed her in the next moment. She melted into the embrace and bathed in his rich scent of fir trees and moss drying in the sun after a rain.

When he let go, they were in his living room. *Home.*

"I…need some time alone," he said in a husky voice.

"Okay."

He vanished, and she dragged herself up to her old room, where she dropped onto the bed.

****

The warm evening sun greeted her when she woke. She got dressed, armed herself, and climbed out the window. With little effort, she reached the roof of the building, where she found a comfortable spot to watch the last rays of the sun. Red and orange colors dyed the sky and offered an incredible view. Before the last remnants of the day vanished below the horizon, Cain appeared behind her.

"What are you doing?" he asked.

"On the off chance I die tonight, I wanted to watch the sunset one last time."

He sighed. "So you're still bent on throwing your life away."

"I'm not throwing it away." She stood up and met his gaze. "Instead, I'm putting it on the line for my dream. Then again, if you're so worried about my life, you can just agree to turn me."

"Nice try. I won't. You can't persuade me, and you won't win in a fight against me." He spoke with an urgency in his voice.

"Don't underestimate me. I'll fight you right now if you're ready."

"I'll never be ready for what you're asking me to do. But since you're not giving me another option, let's get it over with."

Within seconds, she had her staff ready. "Let's begin."

He eyed her skeptically. "Do you intend to fight up here?"

"Why not? Are you scared I'll fall and kill myself? Don't worry, I'm used to heights."

The roof restricted their movements, giving her an advantage. Besides, she'd done worse stunts when she performed at the circus.

"I'm not fighting up here."

Cain offered her his hand and waited until she reluctantly took it. He teleported them to a meadow a few hundred meters from his house. As soon as they arrived, she put some distance between them and spun her staff.

"I hope you've run out of excuses now," she said. "Let's get started."

"It's your funeral."

His eyes grew cold, and all emotion vanished from his face when he drew his sword. He came at her, attacking with several powerful strikes. She deflected each of them with her spinning staff, forcing him to change his pace each time.

"You got an interesting defense," he commented.

The next time he struck, she let her staff clash with his sword, using both of her hands for a forceful counterattack.

"I've got more than a good defense now." She grinned.

"Maybe, but will it be enough?" He put even more force behind his sword, strengthened his grip by using both hands, and pushed her back a few steps.

As a pushing match against him was not in her best interest, she sidestepped him, moved her staff out of his path, swung around, and tried to hit him from behind. Her sudden change of direction caused him to stumble, and she landed a hit on his back before he caught himself.

From then on, he paid more attention to her movements. She stayed on the offensive, assailing him with several fast strikes of her staff. He blocked each of them with his sword, but she pushed him back. With her relentless succession of long-range attacks, she didn't give him a chance to regain the upper hand. Eventually, she had him cornered with his back against a tree.

"Impressive," he said. "Maybe I need to resort to my full power."

The air surrounding him buzzed with electricity as

his supernatural energy multiplied. She retreated a step. Even though she knew he'd been holding back, the full extent of his power intimidated her.

"Who underestimated whom?" he asked. "You can still give up, and we'll forget about it. What do you say?"

"I'll never give up!"

She'd known the risk of facing him. Even if he was stronger than she'd expected, she wouldn't back down. With the power of many outstanding vampires flowing in her veins and her dream right in front of her, she could not capitulate. She'd walk this road to the end, even if it meant her death. And she'd die with no regrets.

Drawing new courage from her conviction, she charged at him. He blocked her attacks and went on the offensive, pushing her back. The next time she blocked his strike, she put both hands on her staff and pushed against him with full force. Subsequently, she let go of her weapon, ducked under his sword, and threw herself into him, causing both of them to fall. Straddling him, she tried to pin him to the ground.

"Do you think you can keep me down?" he scoffed.

He didn't wait for an answer. Letting go of his sword, he took hold of her and rolled both of them until he was on top. When she kicked at him, he let go and got to his feet. She'd disarmed him, although she wondered if this truly put her in a better position. Then again, she hadn't spent countless hours in weaponless fights against Laurant for nothing.

When combining her hand-to-hand combat skills with her swift, controlled moves and her heightened ability to foresee Cain's movements, she didn't do too bad against him. She blocked his punches and kicks while landing a few hits herself.

And yet, the high level of concentration and control of her body, which she needed to keep up with him, took its toll. After a while, her punches became less precise, and his attacks penetrated her defense. He kicked her hard in the ribs. Breathing heavily, she jumped away from him to regain focus.

"You're one of the strongest opponents I've ever faced," he admitted. "It's not enough, though. You can fight at my level temporarily, but you can't keep it up."

"I'm well aware of my limits." She panted. "But I won't surrender. I'll fight till my last breath."

"I see." He overcame the distance between them in a split second.

She blocked his punch, but he kept attacking. Each hit was harder than the last, and soon, even blocking became painful. In order to keep him at a distance, she pulled out her silver-coated whip. She slashed at him, and the tip of the whip bored into his flesh, but he ignored the pain.

Using her desperate position to his advantage, he threw himself at her, pushed her back several steps, and pinned her against a tree. He left her no chance to break free, as he pressed his body against hers and secured her wrists with his hands above her head.

"It's over." His voice was void of emotion.

Chapter 33

After trying to struggle free with no success, Lilah acknowledged her defeat. She quit fighting.

The unfamiliar chill in Cain's eyes sent a shudder down her spine. She closed hers and took a deep breath. If death was her fate, she'd accept it. She'd neither die in fear nor beg for her life. At least he'd be the one who took it.

She opened her eyes again and met his gaze. "It's all right. Do it."

He lowered his head to her neck. After a moment of hesitation, his fangs sank into her flesh.

His bite hurt. She didn't feel the familiar numbness or pleasure. She also didn't feel sleepy or like losing consciousness. Why did he make her suffer in her last moments? Something was off. His bite felt more intense than all the other vampire bites she'd experienced.

After he'd taken several deep pulls of her blood, her heartbeat slowed, and her senses diminished. Before long, she could not see, could not hear, could not smell, could not taste, could not feel, or perceive anything except for pain and the blood leaving her system. And yet she didn't lose consciousness. She felt trapped inside her own body.

Darkness, pain, and suffering—*was this what death was like?* She'd imagined seeing her life flash in front of her eyes one last time or heading toward a light. Instead, there was nothing. Nothing except for agony.

Even when the feeling of blood leaving her system disappeared and the pain subsided, she found no relief. The all-encompassing emptiness was suffocating, and the constant darkness terrorized her.

Soon, she longed to feel anything, even pain.

More time passed. Trapped in an endless state of despair, she lost all sense of who or what she was.

****

A liquid entered her realm of consciousness and crept through the void. Wherever it flowed, pain followed. But she didn't mind the pain. She welcomed it. Pain equaled life, and life was good.

As the liquid spread, so did the pain. Everything felt like it was on fire. Through the pain and the burning sensation, she regained a sense of her body.

The liquid kept flowing, and her limbs reawakened little by little. After a while, she could discern her toes, her feet, her legs, her arms, her hands, and her torso. Every part of her body tingled and burned. Nothing had ever felt more real. Yet she did not know why she felt this way, or what was happening.

When her bubble of consciousness seemed too small, she shifted her focus outward.

The life-giving liquid was blood. Someone was feeding it to her through her mouth. Unlike all the times before, her body longed for more.

Her sense of taste returned, and what she tasted was delicious. She craved more of this exquisite flavor. Letting the blood flow didn't suffice any longer. She sucked it into her system.

Then her sense of smell kicked in. The blood smelled mouthwatering, not metallic like before, but rich and intoxicating. There was also another scent, something or someone familiar, but she couldn't place it.

Her sense of hearing came back next. She heard the blood flow from her mouth through her body and how her heart struggled to distribute it.

After a while, she realized she saw nothing because her lids covered her eyes. She blinked them open. It took her a moment to focus and another moment to put a name to the face in front of her.

Cain was kneeling by her side with a look of relief. He was feeding his blood to her. But why? It didn't make any sense. She'd fought him and lost. Then he'd killed her. Or had he?

She concentrated on her body. It still tingled, but the pain had subsided. Her senses were in overdrive. She was lying on the ground, aware of every blade of grass touching her skin. She was also still sucking his luscious blood. Why had she hated the taste until now? And why wasn't his wound closing? Was she biting into his wrist?

She focused on his face again. Apart from relief, there was curiosity and wonder. She wanted to ask what was happening, but she needed to release his wrist to speak. The thought didn't seem very appealing.

"Even though you enjoy the taste now, I'd really appreciate it if you let go before sucking me dry. My arm's already numb," he said with a wry smile.

It took her some willpower to open her mouth and release his wrist. He pressed his other hand to the wound to stop the bleeding while she gulped down the last drops of blood.

"What happened?" Her voice sounded foreign to her ears.

He stared at her, and his expression twisted until a

troubled smile appeared. "Against my better judgment, I fulfilled your wish and brought you back as a vampire."

"Why?" she asked after letting his announcement sink in. "Don't get me wrong, I'm thrilled. But I lost our duel. So…what changed your mind?"

He averted his gaze. "You should worry about other things now, like getting a hang of your new power, your urges, and your body."

"Don't I have eternity for that?"

He sighed. "I might as well confess. Even though I couldn't admit it to myself, I decided on turning you the moment I laid eyes on you last night."

She frowned. "You did? Why did you fight me, then?"

"Let me elaborate to answer your question. After leaving you, it took me a while to figure out what our time together meant, and I realized I didn't want to live without you. When I came to check on you over a year and a half ago, I'd planned to take you back if you still wanted me. But I assumed the worst when I saw your mother mourn. I thought my stubbornness had cost me everything, and it devastated me.

"So, when our paths crossed again, I knew I could never risk losing you to death for real. Even if I pushed back my feelings and disappeared from your life, you'd die one day. It's selfish, but reality without you is unacceptable to me. And yet, creating another vampire goes against everything I believe in, so I tricked myself.

"A fight for your life was what I needed. I brought you to the brink of death by suppressing my feelings and convincing myself you were just another target. When it was too late to save your life, I let my emotions back in. Since I could not bear losing you, turning you was my only option."

She listened to his speech with an amused grin. "You know you're rambling, right? What was your real reason for turning me?" She knew the answer, but she yearned to hear him say it.

His cheeks flushed as he smiled at her. "I love you."

Chapter 34

Everything clicked into place, and for the first time in her existence, Lilah felt nothing but happiness.

"I love you, too," she whispered.

She lifted her upper body and leaned in to kiss Cain, but her body reacted much faster than she expected, and she almost bumped into him.

He chuckled and pressed a light kiss to her lips before getting to his feet. "Let's do first things first. Getting accustomed to your body should be at the top of your list."

Even though it only lasted two seconds, her lips still tingled from his soft kiss. It was too much and, at the same time, not enough. Everything felt more intense.

She took in her surroundings with an open mouth. "It's the middle of the night, yet I perceive every detail. With millions of stars illuminating this meadow, I can make out every single needle on these fir trees. Hell, I can hear bugs crawling beneath the leaves on the ground. How do you live without being constantly amazed by everything?"

He laughed. "You'll get used to it. As I told you before, there comes a lot of bad with the good. It balances out."

"I doubt anything could spoil this incredible feeling. Although I'm only sitting here, I've never felt so much at once. Does every new vampire feel this way?"

"No, presumably not. You consumed powerful blood before I turned you, and my blood had never been used to sire another vampire, which makes it extremely potent. Thus, you're stronger, and you experience everything more intensely than most young vampires. How did you convince the king to feed you his blood, anyway?"

She glanced away. Had he seen her memories while drinking her blood?

"No, I haven't," he responded to her thought.

She froze. Since when did he possess the ability to read minds?

"Sorry," he said. "I didn't mean to—I wasn't even trying. Your thoughts are flowing into my mind because we're connected. Since you're overwhelmed, they are all over the place. You'll be able to keep them to yourself soon, don't worry. And I know about the king's blood because I tasted his power while feeding on you. It wasn't the only powerful blood I tasted, but I couldn't put names to your other donors."

"I'd appreciate it if you didn't try too hard to find out more about them. They took me in, shared their life with me, and helped me become stronger. Most of them wished to keep their identities hidden." She avoided his gaze. Keeping secrets wasn't the best way to resume their relationship.

"It's okay." He smiled gently at her. "I admire your loyalty, and I won't pry secrets from your mind if I can help it. However, if you wish to tell me about your experiences and the past two years, I'll listen. The king's blood is a matter we have to discuss, though. He doesn't offer it to anyone without a reason, so I wonder what he's planned for you."

"Or us," she said. "He told me I'd complement you and there was nothing we couldn't achieve together. Do you know what he meant?"

"I'm afraid to find out. But considering his last order, we will soon enough. You need to get used to your body before we pay him another visit."

She nodded and took a few steps. "I feel like a kid seeing the world for the first time."

"You are." He smiled fondly. "You've been reborn as a vampire. Let's test your limits. Catch me!"

He ran deeper into the forest, but she didn't react to his challenge. She spotted an ant on the ground and found it fascinating to watch. Although she stood a few meters from the insect, she caught every movement of its tiny legs as it carried a piece of leaf. When it disappeared into an anthill, she diverted her focus back to her sire and scampered after him.

Her feet barely touched the ground as she moved effortlessly through the woods, almost like a bird soaring through the sky. As soon as she caught up to Cain, she jumped, threw her arms around him, and caused both of them to topple to the ground.

"Got you." Warmth radiated through her body as she kissed him.

He gave in to her kiss for just a moment before pushing her away. "Now's not the time. Come on, please focus."

"Why? We've been apart for so long."

"I know." The smile vanished from his lips. "But right now, learning to deal with your emotions takes priority. You're overwhelmed, and everything amazes and tempts you. Like a child, you react to every impulse. Your behavior would be fine if you *were* a child, but you're much more powerful. The urge to feed will emerge soon, and if you don't have a handle on yourself by then, I'm worried what might happen."

She pouted. "Spoilsport."

He was right, though, so she tried to calm her mind. Remembering a meditation technique Daniel had taught her, she plopped down on the ground and concentrated on her body. After focusing on each of her limbs, from her toes to her head, she was in control and much more aware of the power flowing through her veins.

Cain watched her exercise with interest. "Very good. Your thoughts have hushed down considerably. Don't forget you've got eternity to do, feel, and experience everything, so take it slow, okay?"

She stood up and bowed to him to show her respect. Even if he didn't care for her formal gesture, she did. "I trust your judgment, and I'll try to follow your lead and keep my emotions in check. Everything I've ever dreamed of is right here, and I got a little carried away. I'll prove to you I can handle my power, so you don't have to worry." Since he'd fulfilled her deepest desire, easing his mind was the least she could do.

Her speed, strength, and endurance were on par with Cain's. Her senses had heightened to an extent where she needed to learn how to limit her perception so as not to drown in the stimuli. As dawn loomed on the horizon, they postponed the lesson to the next day.

"Since your body is still adjusting, you better avoid the sun for a while." He led her into the basement. "Let's move into my underground bedroom for now."

"Okay." *So he does have a bedroom hidden down here!*

He removed the tapestry from the back wall of the

fitness and weapons room to reveal a fireproof door. She followed him into the hidden room, which contained a big box bed with purple satin sheets. Two bedside tables and a wardrobe with a mirror front completed the furnishings. There were no windows or decorations on the stone walls. A second door led to a bathroom with a shower, toilet, and washbasin.

"Do I still need to use the toilet?"

"Sometimes…Especially if you consume human beverages. Your body excretes whatever it can't use."

She viewed herself in the mirror. Dirt and dried blood covered her body. "I definitely need to take a shower, though. I look like a mess."

"Go ahead." He chuckled. "I'll get you fresh clothes from upstairs."

The stream of water dripping down her body felt amazing. Every drop caressed her skin like a lover's soft touch. After showering, she dried off and left the small bathroom. He had put a nightgown and panties out for her, but she lost all interest in putting on clothes the moment she saw him. He was lying on the bed, wearing nothing but boxer shorts. Images of taking advantage of their lack of clothes flooded her mind.

"Don't tempt me with your thoughts." He grinned. "In your current state, I'd overwhelm you with sensations."

"Sounds good to me."

He shrugged. "You've already proven remarkable control today, and we're safe in here, so I guess there's no harm in—"

She dived into his arms before he'd finished his sentence. "I yearn to feel you…to know this is not a dream."

"Oh, this is real." He flipped her around so she was lying beneath him on the bed. She looked straight into his wild, passionate eyes. They swept her away like a tsunami wave. "I'll prove it to you."

Even his simplest touch felt incredible. He let his hands wander along her skin before settling on her bare breasts, tormenting her with small, circular movements. Without warning, he took her taut nipples between his fingertips and tugged sharply. The intense stimulation elicited a cry of pleasure from her.

"It's almost too easy," he gasped. "Our connection allows me to revel in what you're feeling as well."

Her hands explored his body, and she clawed at his boxer shorts to remove them. "Then you know it's not enough," she panted.

"Careful, or I might lose the last of my self-control." He claimed her mouth in a raw kiss.

"Lose it." Her body throbbed with desire, and she pulled him even closer so his naked skin pressed against hers. "Give me all of you."

"I already am yours." His voice was a sexy growl.

Her chest fluttered at his words. "And I am yours, so…take me."

He grabbed the back of her knees to spread her legs apart. She relinquished all control as he thrust into her, and euphoria drowned everything else. One sensation after the other flooded her body and mind, and she lost herself in the sensory overload.

Chapter 35

A gnawing hunger tore Lilah from her sleep. But the word "hunger" didn't even begin to describe what she felt. Every cell inside her body screamed, and she had trouble forming a clear thought. Where was Cain? When she called his name, he appeared next to her, wearing fresh clothes.

"What is happening to me?" She clutched her hands to her stomach. "It feels like someone is twisting a knife in my belly."

"Your body is hurting for blood," he said. "Get dressed, then we'll find you a donor."

She finished dressing even before he picked out a coat. "Let's go," she urged him on. Only the promise of pain relief kept her sane.

"I hoped to work more on your self-restraint and focus before going among humans." He grimaced as he offered her his hand. "Since we don't have the time, a remote area with only a few people around will have to do."

She held on to him, and he teleported them to a country road leading through a small village. Less than a hundred meters from their location, a couple was out on a late-night walk.

"Choosing a lone victim might be the safer bet, but you're too hungry to wait, and it'll get worse with time. On the plus side, after all the blood I gave you, I should feed as well. Try to follow my lead and remember humans are fragile. You're not aware of your own strength, so imagine handling a raw egg when interacting with them."

She nodded, although she didn't grasp what he told her. Hunger dominated her thoughts and made it impossible to concentrate.

He sneaked up on the female victim, grabbed her from behind, and bit into her neck. She imitated him, burying her fangs into the man's neck a couple of seconds later. The act felt natural. The man cried out in pain, but she didn't know how to ease his suffering. She stopped caring as soon as his blood entered her system.

Although a few sips soothed the horrible hunger, they didn't suffice. No amount of blood would ever satisfy her. The more she drank, the more her body longed for this rich taste. Nothing compared to the pleasurable warmth spreading through her body as she thrived on the man's life. Lost in the sensation, she didn't even notice his whimpering.

Cain ripped the man from her grasp and pushed her to the ground.

"Lilah, focus!" he shouted.

She blinked, taking in the scene. The woman lay sleeping against a fence. Cain held the man in his arms while pressing his bleeding wrist to the man's neck. She hadn't just left a bite mark. She'd torn his throat open. A wave of guilt hit her.

"Don't worry, he'll be fine," Cain said. "With my blood, he'll be back to normal in no time. And I'll make sure he won't remember being attacked."

She nodded. Without him, she'd have killed the poor man without even realizing what she did. The prospect paralyzed her.

When he approached her a minute later, she was rocking back and forth on the ground.

He squatted down in front of her. "Feeding is difficult...Having a human's life in your hands and knowing you might kill him if you lose control...It's terrifying. But you're not alone. I'm with you all the way. I'll teach you to control your lust for blood, and I'll always stop you before you go too far. Okay?"

She didn't look at him. Every emotion felt much more intense, choking her. Terrible emotions like pain, suffering, and shame overshadowed the wonderful ones like amazement, happiness, and pleasure. The weight of almost taking a human's life crushed her.

Cain had often told her about the drawbacks of being a vampire, but she hadn't understood what he'd meant until then. The ungodly desire to consume blood, without caring if her victim suffered or died, frightened her.

"You're strong. You'll be able to control your hunger in no time. I won't let you out of my sight until you've mastered the bloodlust. In time, you'll get used to the good and the bad aspects of being a vampire. As soon as you get a hang of your emotions, the bad things won't be so bad." He tried to give her a reassuring smile.

She nodded again without looking at him.

"Let's get you home for now." He placed his hand on her shoulder and teleported them back.

She snuggled into a blanket on the couch. If it was up to her, she'd stay there, far away from any human she could hurt.

He watched her for a while before flopping down on the couch and pulling her into a tight embrace. "I know how you feel. It'll only get worse if you hide yourself away because you dread the act of feeding. If you don't want the same thing happening again tomorrow, you need to practice on at least one more human tonight. Plus, if you feed more often, the hunger and loss of control will lessen."

Reluctantly, she turned her head to look at him. "Okay…But I don't want to hurt anyone. How do I keep them from feeling pain?"

"I should have explained before letting you feed," he said ruefully. "Do you recall what I told you about the fluids vampires can inject their victims with?"

She nodded. "How do I use them?"

"Most vampires inject them instinctively, so it's hard for me to explain the mechanics. Basically, you have to will it. If you bite someone while wishing they'll fall asleep and forget about the whole incident, it'll happen.

"If you bite with the desire to share the pleasure you feel, they'll feel your pleasure. Your intent will regulate which fluid you inject into your donors and how they'll experience the bite. But for it to work, you require focus and control of your emotions. Always feed before the thirst for blood overwhelms you."

"All right," she said. "Let's practice. I'll try a meditation technique before we leave."

****

An hour later, they walked down a dark alley. The full moon hung high in the sky, and the streets were empty. A girl, no more than seventeen or eighteen years old, was hurrying home. She kept looking over her shoulder and eyed Cain and Lilah warily when she passed them.

"She'll be as good as anyone. And she's young, so

losing some blood won't harm her," he encouraged Lilah.

She took a deep breath. After a quick sprint, she caught up to the girl and grabbed her from behind. The girl cried out and tried to break loose, but she didn't give her a chance to escape. She carefully bit into the girl's neck, willing her to fall asleep. The girl became quiet, and her breathing slowed down as her blood poured into Lilah's mouth. Even though the taste threatened to overwhelm her once again, she tried hard to concentrate on her surroundings and the sound of the girl's breathing.

Cain stood next to her. "Now, imagine a plausible scenario explaining why she'd be lying here on the street. Picture it from her point of view and will the memory into her."

She imagined the girl stumbling and hitting her head. Then she pictured sending the memory into the girl's mind. While she still wondered if her effort worked, Cain's cautioning voice caught her attention.

"You've taken enough blood. Let go of her."

It took her a few moments to release the girl's neck. She inspected her bite marks. Although she hadn't torn into the flesh like last time, she still left quite an injury.

"Heal her," he instructed. She bit into her finger and smeared her blood on the victim's wound. It closed within seconds, leaving unblemished skin behind. She lapped the remaining blood up off the girl's skin before placing her on the ground.

"Good job," he said.

"Not really. Without you, I'd have taken too much blood. And it was a challenge to stop…"

"But you stopped in time and handled her on your own. I only gave you instructions. For your second time feeding, you did extraordinarily well."

His optimism didn't convince her. "I'm not sure I manipulated her memories. How am I supposed to know if I succeeded?"

"It takes practice. Once you're used to drinking blood, you'll sense how you influence your donors. For now, how about we monitor how she reacts once she wakes?"

"I'd like to see her get home."

"Okay. Let's watch her from afar."

They climbed on top of the town houses flanking the alley and observed her from above.

The girl woke up twenty minutes later. She seemed disoriented at first and felt her head for an injury. After a minute or two, she stood up and glanced around. Then she ran. They followed her until she entered a house two streets from where they'd assaulted her.

"Satisfied?" he asked.

She nodded, breathing a sigh of relief. Seeing the girl get home safely lifted a weight off her shoulders.

Chapter 36

Lilah strolled along the dike of a port she'd often visited as a child. Wind blew her hair across her face, and even though the frosty air cut into her cheeks, she cherished feeling the forces of nature on her skin. Vampirism allowed her to experience everything more clearly, and she loved it.

A young man passed by, and the scent of vanilla reached her nose. She licked her lips as she turned around and called after him. "Excuse me?"

He spun around to look at her. "Yes?"

"Didn't we go to school together?" She'd never seen the man before in her life, but the question stalled him. He searched her face for something familiar, and when their eyes locked, she sent him a subconscious command. *Stay calm. Remove your scarf.*

She moved her hands as if removing a nonexistent scarf herself, and he mirrored her gestures, baring his neck in the process. She approached, wrapped her arms around him, and sank her teeth into his throat, numbing the pain immediately. His sweet blood flowed into her mouth while she made him believe he'd slipped on the icy ground and an unknown woman helped him to his feet.

Once his heart quivered, she released him, cut her tongue on her fang, and licked over the bite mark to heal it. Then she took a step back, still supporting him with her arms. "Are you all right? You took a nasty fall there."

The young man blinked at her in confusion. "I…um…yes. Thank you for helping me up."

"You're welcome." She smiled and left him standing on his own. "Have a good night."

She resumed her midnight stroll. After one month, feeding was routine, although knowing Cain never strayed too far from her in case she lost control of her urges played a big part in her progress. As if on cue, he appeared by her side.

"Getting your donor to strip for you…" He chuckled. "I'm glad he stopped at his scarf, though."

She rolled her eyes. "It's not like you exclusively feed on men."

"You know he kept staring at you even after you parted?" He pursed his lips.

She pressed a kiss to his cheek. "You have nothing to worry about. It's just a convenient way of feeding in winter. With their scarves, gloves, and hats, there is nowhere to bite."

He laughed. "You know, most vampires don't have the luxury of preparing their donors telepathically."

"I know." Her cheeks heated. *And I should probably thank Daniel one of these days for the perks I got from his blood.*

"Anyway," Cain started, "how about we get our visit to court over with?"

"Well, we've definitely run out of excuses not to go."

"Come on, then." He offered her his hand. Their fingers intertwined, and he teleported them to the road leading up to the royal castle.

"When will I be able to teleport on my own?" she

asked as they walked side by side.

"I don't know. It took me a few decades to obtain that skill. Considering the power slumbering within you, it wouldn't surprise me if you were already able to. I could explain the mechanics to you, but…if you teleport somewhere without me, you'll be on your own. Are you ready for that?"

"I'll be fine. I can control my emotions now." She grinned. "Sounds to me like you're having trouble letting me out of your sight, though."

He glared at her.

"Don't worry, I won't run from you," she added teasingly.

"Let's talk about this later. We're almost at the castle, so…maybe you should behave accordingly?" His lips pressed into a thin line. They were just a few meters from the front entrance.

"As you wish," she said with a quick bow and a smirk. She knew being at court agitated him.

A guard led them inside and announced their presence. They approached the king and kneeled down about five meters from him. As Cain was her sire, she stayed behind him.

The king greeted them with a wide grin. "It's good to see you two."

Cain bowed his head. "As requested, I'm here to present Lilah as my fledgling, Your Majesty."

"Has she won against you? And if not, what changed your mind?" the king asked.

"She's powerful, but she was human when she challenged me. So, no, she lost. Since eternity without her seemed dull, I decided to keep her around."

The king nodded with a knowing smile. Then he

addressed her. "So, Lilah…Is vampirism everything you'd hoped for?"

"Some things are more challenging than I'd imagined. But after getting the hang of feeding and controlling my emotions, I can say I love being a vampire, Your Majesty."

"Why did you request our presence, Your Majesty? Surely it wasn't to see how Lilah is handling her transformation?"

"It's part of the reason. I want to make both of you an offer."

"An offer?" Cain furrowed his brows. She listened quietly. It wasn't her place to ask questions.

"I want the two of you to join the royal family. It's not a far stretch since both of you already consumed royal blood," the king explained.

"Why?" she blurted out against her better judgment.

The king smiled at her. "You're young, and it's an important decision, so feel free to ask questions. As of now, the royal family consists of Lucious and me. Our blood is powerful, and our power speaks for itself, but there are vampires who don't respect or who oppose us. I wish to strengthen our position by welcoming you to the family."

"Why us? I've only been a vampire for a few weeks," she said.

"Yet you're already one of the most powerful vampires I've met. You may be young and inexperienced, but Cain isn't. The two of you together are an ideal addition."

"What if we're not interested?" Cain asked.

The king turned to him. "It's an offer, so you can refuse. I know you won't enjoy the fame and responsibilities which the position entails. You're not ambitious, and you don't care enough about our people. You care about Lilah, though. She's ambitious enough for both of you and eager to take whatever she can get. She'll be reaching for the stars while you keep her grounded. You're a perfect combination."

"What does your offer mean for our everyday life?" she asked.

"Your life won't change unless you want it to," the king replied. "It's mostly a symbolic position. You'd have the authority of the court, though. And if something happened to me and Lucious, you'd be the rightful heirs to the throne. Until then, you can keep living your life. If you wish to continue going on assignments, bringing down hunters, and taking care of other threats to our people, you'd simply do it in a more official capacity."

"I doubt my sire would appreciate a change in my status," Cain remarked.

"I've discussed my offer with Lucious. He doesn't mind, since he'll still be next in line. Besides, if you plotted against him, it would be treason and result in you losing your right to the throne."

"How long have you been planning this?" Cain growled.

"What are you implying?" the king returned the question.

"You didn't come up with such an offer on a whim. So, when did you know?"

The king sighed. "You and I both know the future is a fickle thing...But I had an inkling the first time I looked into her blood."

"What are you saying?" she asked.

"I can't only see the past in someone's blood.

Sometimes, I'm allowed glimpses of the future as well."

She held her breath. "So you *knew…*"

"Yes. I saw this very moment when I tasted your blood to find out if Cain was telling the truth about Lucious kidnapping you."

"Why didn't you…"

"What? Tell you all your wishes would come true, and thus rob you of your ambition?" The king shook his head. "Knowing the future can be a curse. And there's no guarantee it won't change."

She swallowed. She might not have gone on her journey and befriended so many vampires if she'd known. Looking back, she wouldn't trade her memories for anything in the world.

"So…" He cleared his throat. "What do you think about my offer?"

"We need to discuss this matter privately," Cain chipped in.

"Very well. Take all the time you need. I'll await your decision."

They bid him farewell and left the throne hall.

Lucious appeared the moment they exited through the main gate. As expected of him, Cain went down on his knee and bowed his head. She followed his example.

Lucious eyed her with interest. "Has your little pet actually brought you down?"

"What are you talking about?" Cain asked.

"Oh, just a rumor I've heard…" Lucious smirked.

"I couldn't defeat him," she admitted in a whisper.

"How disappointing." Lucious' eyes narrowed on her. "But still an interesting development."

He entered the castle, leaving Cain and Lilah behind.

Elli Morgan

****

"Care to explain how Lucious knew about my prerequisite for turning you? I doubt the king told him." Cain interrogated her back at home.

"I sought Lucious out when I couldn't find any other powerful vampires." She averted her gaze.

"Are you insane?" he asked, fear filling his voice.

"I knew it might have ended badly, but desperation led me to him."

"Badly? He might have killed you or tortured you for years. Why did you put yourself in such a position?"

She flinched at his accusation. "You'd abandoned me. I'd been traveling through Europe for more than a month, and the only vampires I'd stumbled upon were weak fledglings. Lucious was the sole more-or-less-powerful vampire whose location I knew. I had nothing to lose, so I tried my luck."

"Nothing to lose? What about your life?"

She pursed her lips.

"It wasn't the only risk you've taken, eh?" His eyebrows drew together.

"No, it wasn't. I thought I'd die more than once on my journey. And yet I survived, and I'd do it all again, since it brought me to where I am right now."

"I was afraid you'd say that."

"It's all worked out for the best, so stop worrying." She pressed a kiss to his lips.

Chapter 37

"Are we going to discuss the king's offer?" Lilah asked the next evening as Cain played a joyful melody on the piano.

"Depends. Are you interested in taking his offer?" His fingers halted on the keys mid-song.

She leaned on the piano to meet his gaze. "Royalty sounds tempting, doesn't it?"

"It doesn't to me. I hate obligations and formalities, and they'll be hard to avoid if we're part of the royal family."

"I only know of the formal interactions based on hierarchy. What other obligations are there?"

"There are a lot of formal events, for example, balls and ceremonies."

"Well, I'd love to attend a ball sometime. And being king and queen of all vampires has a certain ring to it, doesn't it?" she fantasized.

He shook his head. "With the title comes responsibility. The king deals with people and other matters all night long. I have no interest in ruling over anyone. I prefer my quiet life and going on a hunt now and then."

"You wouldn't be on your own. With the two of us, I'm sure we could share the responsibilities so they wouldn't tie us down. Besides, I doubt it'll ever come to that anyway," she argued.

He chuckled. "You don't have a concept of how long forever lasts and how much can change with time."

"Well, we can deal with it when we get there."

"So you want to accept?"

She nodded. "But…this decision affects both of us. And how can I ask you to go along with my wish when you've already sacrificed so much for me?"

"What do you mean?"

"You never wanted to turn a human, and I forced you to discard your principles."

He stared at her. "It may have been your wish, but I fulfilled it for my own selfish desires." His eyes turned into an ocean filled with love. "I can't imagine spending even one more lifetime without you. You see me like no one ever has, and I need you to continue seeing me through your beautiful eyes. Will you do that?"

"Always."

"Then I'll always support you, no matter where your path leads you."

"Us," she corrected him.

"Us." He planted a tender kiss on her lips. "But please, ponder the offer a little longer before making any hasty decisions, okay? You've got all the time in the world."

"All right." She smiled. "In the meantime, why don't you divulge to me how teleportation works?"

"Fine." He sighed. "It requires a high level of concentration. Picture yourself in the place you want to teleport to. Imagine how it makes you feel and any smells and sounds you associate with it. Once you've pictured everything, you have to will your body there. Because of the required details, you can only teleport to places you've visited before. In the beginning, it'll be easier for you to teleport to somewhere important to you. With time and practice, you'll be able to return to any place."

"Sounds easy enough," she said.

"If you think so, try it."

When she closed her eyes to concentrate, he added, "Picture another room in this house for your first try. I'd rather not have to look all over the globe for you in case something goes wrong and you end up somewhere far away with no idea how to return."

"All right," she grumbled. She'd already imagined another place, but he was right. Thus, she pictured her old room on the second floor of his house. As soon as she saw every detail in her mind, she willed her body upstairs. After several seconds, she opened her eyes.

"I can teleport!" she exclaimed happily.

Nothing stopped her from trying a longer-distance teleportation next.

"I'll give it another go," she shouted loud enough for him to hear. "Don't worry about me. I'm sure I'll find my way back somehow."

"Lilah, wait!" he yelled from downstairs.

She ignored him. With her destination in mind, she vanished.

****

The smell of popcorn and the familiar rumble of circus workers cleaning up after a show greeted her.

"Lilah!" a familiar voice shouted.

Footsteps ran up to her, and arms wrapped around her waist from behind. She shuddered as her friend's warmth and vitality stirred her primal instincts. Maybe she hadn't thought her trip through too well. Interacting with humans was a different matter than feeding from them.

"Vanessa, how are you?" She greeted her friend with a stiff smile, but she didn't dare return the girl's hug. Humans were fragile.

Vanessa beamed at her. "I'm great! Did you watch our performance? I tried a new act today."

She shook her head. "Sorry, no. I need to talk to Sophie."

"Awwww, what a pity." Vanessa pouted. "How about joining us for a drink?"

"I can't," she said. She didn't want to tempt fate by surrounding herself with so many humans.

"Well, who do we have here?" another familiar voice said.

Lilah turned around to see Lexi. After berating herself for not noticing a vampire walking up to her, she relaxed. "Hey! You're the person I was looking for. Can we speak somewhere privately?"

Lexi nodded. "Let's talk in my trailer."

Before following Lexi, she turned to Vanessa. "I'll visit soon with more time. Then I'll join you guys for a drink, all right?"

"Sure. See ya," Vanessa said, with a hint of disappointment in her voice.

Lexi was already sitting on a couch in her trailer when she entered.

"Thanks, you saved me," Lilah said.

"Being among a group of humans takes some getting used to. It'll get easier with time, though. And from what I can see, you've got plenty of time. Did everything work out the way you'd planned?"

"More or less. Although I couldn't defeat him, he turned me. It's been over a month now, and I'm still adjusting. Some things are challenging, but I'm happy."

"I'm glad you're happy." Lexi smiled. "How did you end up here tonight?"

"I teleported!" She beamed, lifting her chin high. "It was my second try and an excellent opportunity to visit and talk to you without my sire fussing over me."

Her friend chuckled. "What do you wish to talk about?"

"The king asked us—my sire and me—to join the royal family," she said, and Lexi's eyes widened. "I'm not sure I understand the significance of his offer. My sire doesn't want the responsibilities, and it biases his opinion. I hope you can give me another perspective."

Lexi gaped at her. "I know you're strong, and I figured your sire is strong, too…But how on earth did you get the king to make you such an offer?"

"My sire has close connections with the royal family, so I already met the king and the prince as a human." She didn't mention she'd fed on the king's blood before. Judging by her friend's reaction, the implications were much bigger than she'd presumed.

"You'd be the first female vampire joining the royal family in more than a millennium. Until now, no one has ever recognized a female member of the court for her own power. They've only ever been the companions of kings or princes. So, if the king offered you this position because of your talent, it'd be a first. You'd be a role model. Then again, a lot of vampires will challenge your status, especially because you're young."

"Wow, there's much more to this than I assumed…"

"Don't let it discourage you—I know you'll do great."

"Thanks." Lilah hugged her. "I knew you'd tell me

what I needed to hear. I better return to my sire now…He's probably worried sick."

"Anytime. I hope I'll see you soon."

She took a step back, closed her eyes, and concentrated. When she opened them again, she stood in Cain's living room. "I'm back!"

He appeared in front of her within seconds. "Are you okay? Where have you been?"

"I paid a quick visit to a friend, who helped me decide. Joining the royal family is an opportunity I cannot miss. I'm sure the two of us will rise to any challenge, so…let's do it?"

"Are you absolutely sure you want this and everything it entails?"

"Yes. And you know me—once I've made up my mind, I stick to it."

"True." His eyes brightened as they met hers. "I'll let the king know."

Chapter 38

"Why do we have to dress up?" Lilah complained. She wore a simple but elegant black silk dress going down to her ankles. Although the soft material caressed her skin, she felt exposed, and she hated every step she took in her high heels.

"You asked for this." Cain raised an eyebrow as his eyes absorbed her. "And you shouldn't be the one complaining."

She took another look at his black Victorian swallowtail and laughed. "I expected something else when you said formal attire. How many vampires will witness us dressed this way tonight?"

"There are roughly four and a half thousand vampires living in Europe. Most of them are rather young and weak, so they won't find their way to the castle. Some vampires don't care about what's happening at court, and some aren't welcome here. All things considered, I predict around two hundred guests tonight."

She gulped. "I've performed in front of hundreds of humans, but I dread standing in front of a crowd of vampires…"

"Relax. You don't have to perform tonight." He squeezed her hand. "It's time to go."

They left the dressing room and walked to the throne hall. When they entered side by side, the room fell silent, and every head turned to them. She kept her eyes focused on the king and Lucious, who sat on their respective thrones, wearing old-fashioned ball garments.

On her way to the front of the hall, she glanced at the crowd. Her stomach roiled as hundreds of eyes stared at them. Cain had underestimated the number of vampires attending the ceremony.

The first familiar face Lilah made out was Lexi's. Her friend beamed at her. She also spotted Damian, Laurant, and several vampires she'd fought during her time at the fight club. When their eyes met for a second, Laurant greeted her with a nod.

The familiar faces from her journey filled her with confidence. She wasn't among strangers. She was right where she belonged.

They arrived at the front and kneeled down three meters from the thrones, their heads bowed.

The king rose to speak. "Welcome, my people, children of eternity. I'm overjoyed to see how many of you have come to witness these two join the ranks of the royal family tonight. In fact, I haven't seen so many vampires at court since my coronation. Curiosity brought many of you here. Maybe you've heard rumors about them. Maybe you know one or both of them. In case you don't, let me formally introduce them to you now."

He approached Lilah and Cain, stopped right in front of them, and put his hand on Cain's head. "This is Cain, first child of Lucious. Born to darkness in 1622. He's worked as an enforcer for the court for centuries."

He put his other hand on Lilah's head. "And this young one is Lilah, first child of Cain. Born to darkness just at the end of last year. Despite her age, she's blessed with remarkable talent and strength. Through sheer ambition, she brought down powerful vampires even before she became one herself. I'm confident these two will help our nation prosper, so I offer them my blood tonight. Drink, my children, and become part of my family."

With these words, he let his hands sink, turning them so his palms faced upward. Lilah and Cain slowly leaned forward and bit into the wrist the king offered each of them. They took several deep pulls of the king's blood before letting go at the same time.

"It is done," the king announced.

The spectators greeted them with applause.

Epilogue

One and a half years after their accession ceremony, the king summoned Lilah and Cain to court. He'd often requested their presence in the past months. This time, he asked everyone else to leave the throne hall.

As soon as the last guard left and closed the door, she asked, "What's this about, Your Majesty?"

"What do you know about vampires in North America?" the king asked.

"Nothing," she said.

"When humankind explored the world and discovered America, several vampires followed them to the New World. Once the American colonies demanded their independence, the American vampires distanced themselves from us. They refused to recognize the authority of the royal family any longer and built their own hierarchy.

"Back then, traveling to America was only feasible by ship. Most vampires tried to avoid the long and challenging journey, so we let them be. The American and European vampires have coexisted without too much overlap or interaction ever since. All things considered, it's a fragile relationship."

"Thank you for explaining our history," she said. "But why are you telling us about American vampires now?"

"I received a message from the American royal

family last night. They require our help. More precisely, they've asked for our strongest warriors," the king said.

"Why?" Cain asked.

"Do you remember the rumor about American vampires experimenting on human children by feeding them blood and training them?" The king's eyes fixated on Lilah.

"How could I forget?" The rumor had paved the way for everything she'd achieved.

"Apparently, it's much more than a rumor. They've already raised several kids and turned them once they were full-grown. However, the experiment backfired. One of the strongest vampires they've nurtured joined a faction of vampire hunters to fight against her own kind. Even though she's young, she's extremely powerful. Every attempt to bring her and the hunters down has failed."

"Do you want us to travel to the States and take care of her?"

"I couldn't think of anyone more fitting for this task than the two of you." The king smiled at her. "But this is merely the official assignment."

"What do you mean by 'official'?" Cain asked, his eyes narrowing.

"There is an official and an unofficial mission. I want you to travel to the States, find this renegade vampire, and fight against her. Your official mission is to kill her. I don't doubt your ability to bring her down and show the American vampires up. However, if she's as strong as they say, help her instead.

"We've got no quarrel with her. She's doing us a favor by going after American vampires and keeping them weak and scattered. Your unofficial mission is to assist her in her quest to bring the American royal family down. Since I can't have the two of you starting a war, you won't travel as official representatives of the royal family. Will you accept the mission?"

"Of course," they answered in unison. Her stomach fluttered in anticipation of whatever awaited them on this new journey.

A word about the author...

Elli Morgan was born in 1991 in a small town in Germany. Although she only started learning English in sixth grade, she quickly fell in love with the language. To improve her skills, she spent a year working and traveling in Canada and the US.

As a teenager, she devoured countless fanfictions and vampire novels. During that time, she also developed the idea for this book, but she didn't write it down until the COVID-19 lockdown in 2020.

Apart from being a writer, she's also a trained mathematician, working as Business Intelligence Developer at an IT company. In her free time, she enjoys hiking, traveling, and all kinds of games.

For more information, please visit her website at: ellimorgan.com

Thank you for purchasing
this publication of The Wild Rose Press, Inc.

For questions or more information
contact us at
info@thewildrosepress.com.

The Wild Rose Press, Inc.
www.thewildrosepress.com